Across the Steel River

by Ted Stenhouse

Kids Can Press

Kids Can Press acknowledges the financial support of the Ontario Arts Council,
the Canada Council for the Arts and the Government of Canada, through the
BPIDP, for our publishing activity.

Published in Canada by
Kids Can Press Ltd.
29 Birch Avenue
Toronto, ON M4V 1E2

Published in the U.S. by
Kids Can Press Ltd.
2250 Military Road
Tonawanda, NY 14150

www.kidscanpress.com

Edited by Charis Wahl
Interior designed by Stacie Bowes
Cover designed by Marie Bartholomew

Printed and bound in Canada
This book is smyth sewn casebound.

CM 01 0 9 8 7 6 5 4 3 2 1

Canadian Cataloguing in Publication Data

Stenhouse, Ted
        Across the Steel River

ISBN 1-55074-891-2

I. Title.

PS8587.T4485A83 2001   jC813'.6   C00-932879-3
PZ7.S73Ac 2001

Kids Can Press is a Nelvana company

To my wife and daughter, Faine and Teya:
for encouragement and innocence,
for patience and trust, for love and joy.

Grayson and Its Surroundings

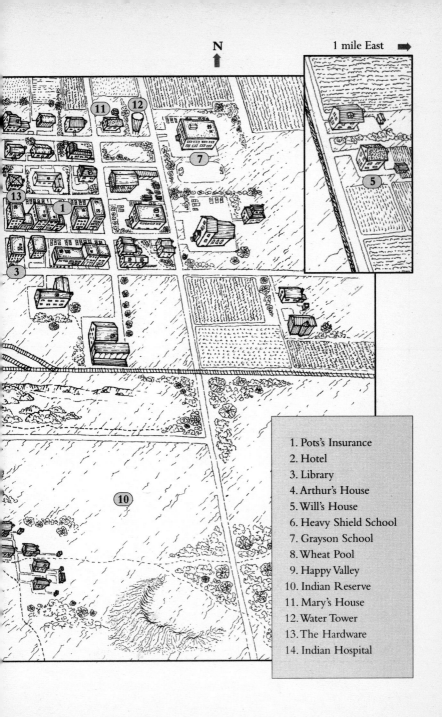

N

1 mile East ➡

1. Pots's Insurance
2. Hotel
3. Library
4. Arthur's House
5. Will's House
6. Heavy Shield School
7. Grayson School
8. Wheat Pool
9. Happy Valley
10. Indian Reserve
11. Mary's House
12. Water Tower
13. The Hardware
14. Indian Hospital

There's a Body in Happy Valley

When we first saw it, I thought it was a dog, but Arthur said it was a man.

He sounded like he thought I didn't know anything about anything. If I hadn't been so scared, I would've been mad. Instead, I stood with my mouth open, breathing in jerky breaths like I was getting ready to run.

My tongue was as dry as road dirt.

"Maybe it's Mr. Norman's black Lab," I said, and tried to swallow.

Arthur shook his head as he gazed two hundred yards down the tracks into the dirt hollow on that narrow strip of railway land between the town and the reserve.

There it lay, curled away from us, still, in the heavy layer of dust at the bottom of the hollow.

I pulled on Arthur's shirttail and tipped my head toward the alley that ran behind the butcher shop. "We could go around the train station, then cut through town."

Arthur gave me a smart look as he puffed out his breath.

"What was that for?"

"You're awfully scared of a dog."

"I'm not scared of nothing."

"Okay," he said, and started walking.

I looked down the alley and followed. We kept to the railway tracks till we passed the station house and got to where the one track changed into three. I had my head turned to the right and was acting like I was interested in the new Dodge cars and Fargo trucks Mr. Gunther had for sale.

"I like the new 1952s," I said to Arthur's back. "I mean, the '51s were okay last year, I guess. But those '50s looked like they couldn't make up their minds if they wanted to be '49s or '51s." I took a big breath. "What do you think?"

"I think you're as scared as a girl."

I looked away from the row of cars and trucks and watched the back of Arthur's boots as he walked. The closer we got, the more scared I became. At a hundred yards, I stopped.

"Now what?" Arthur asked.

"Maybe it's Father Conner's Saint Bernard. He's a pretty big dog."

Arthur held his hands above his eyes and squinted. "If it is, he's wearing the Father's boots," he said, smirking at me.

"Okay, so it's a man."

Arthur didn't answer, except to get a smug look.

"But he's probably just a drunk," I said.

Arthur took his hands down from shading his eyes. They were narrow and dark, and his face was working its way to a hot red color. "Say what you really mean, Will Samson."

"I mean he's a drunk, is all. You don't need to get mad."

"You mean he's a drunk Indian."

"Come on, Arthur. Let's go snare some gophers." I pulled on his sleeve.

Arthur turned away from me and stood with his back to Grayson and looked into Happy Valley, where the man was lying.

Happy Valley wasn't much more than a dirt hollow made from spring runoff. The grass was all trampled down from walking or rolling around or maybe even fighting. Clumps of Saskatoon bushes grew along the top edge on the reserve side of the hollow. Mixed in the bushes were some tall weeds. On the town side, the ground was open with short, sunburned grass. A dirt path ran through the hollow and out onto the reserve.

"Say what you mean," he said again.

I looked at my feet and the rocks that held the ties and the rails. Arthur was right. I meant the man was a drunk Indian, but it didn't come from my own thoughts so much as hearing a hundred times a day from the people of Grayson that *All Indians are drunks.* And I knew I couldn't say that to Arthur, not because he was an Indian, and not because he would get hurt feelings, but because Arthur was my best friend.

I was getting ready to talk about snaring gophers when the man let out a horrible moan.

Arthur jerked his head toward me — his eyes were big, and his mouth was hanging open. Before the man could moan again, Arthur tore off along the tracks toward Happy Valley.

In a second, I was running after him.

At the Wheat Pool elevator, we turned left off the railway tracks, slid down the mound of rocks that held the ties and rails, and headed along the path.

The moaning grew into loud, miserable cries. The man thrashed and rolled in the dust, then went stiff. The cries faded to quick grunting breaths. There was a gasp. Then nothing.

In another twenty strides, we reached the edge of the hollow. We crossed over, still running hard, our feet making puffs in the heavy dust like little explosions.

Arthur tried to stop, but all he could do was slide in the dust with his arms waving in big circles. A second later, he crashed right into the man with both feet.

I came sliding in and crashed into Arthur.

For a long second we stood there hanging on to each other and looking down. The man was curled up with his back toward us. He was covered in dirt stuck to his body with something wet — maybe it was sweat, but I was afraid it was blood.

"Oh, jeez," Arthur said.

"Is he drunk?" I whispered.

Arthur started to give me a look, then stopped.

"Is he sleeping?"

Arthur made a low mumbling that sounded like he was praying in Indian.

Then the man's head turned slowly, as if he was going to take a sneaky look at us.

I saw the eye first, looking at me, all cloudy like I'd seen a hundred times before in snared gophers.

"*Akaiiniu*," Arthur mumbled.

"I don't understand."

"He's dead."

I jumped back and tripped over my own feet. When I got up, Arthur had already crossed through Happy Valley and was headed down the path toward the reserve.

I ran for town, jumped the three sets of tracks in three long strides, and headed to the Wheat Pool elevator.

Mr. Norman was standing at the top of the ramp watching me as I turned the corner.

Mr. Norman looked like grain ready for harvest. He was tall. His skin was straw colored. His hair was straw colored. And he was so skinny he swayed in a wind.

He pulled out his hankie and gave it a snap. A cloud of chaff flew into the air.

"What's the hurry, lad?" he asked, and wiped his eyes.

I stood in front of him, my mouth half open, with nothing coming out that could pass for words.

"Lord love a duck," he said, blinking after each word. "It looks like you've seen the dead."

"There's a man," I said and pointed. "He's ... He's ..."

"Is he hurt?"

"He's ..." I made a hard, dry swallow. "I think he's dead."

Mr. Norman jerked his head toward the wall where I had just pointed. "Where?" he asked. "Behind the elevator?"

"In Happy Valley. He's just lying there with his eyes open."

"God help us." He rushed to the telephone that hung on the wall. "Gladys," he said into the telephone. "Get me the Mounties. No, hold on, Gladys. You call them yourself. Tell them there's a body behind the Wheat Pool elevator, where the Indians drink."

He looked at me and nodded as he talked. His eyes went round and still for half a second when he said "body." A second later, he was blinking faster than ever.

I stood over the grain screen and started to shake. I saw the eye again. It was staring at me. I tried to look away, but it wasn't in a place I could look away from. It was in my head.

"Yes, that's right, Gladys, Happy Valley. And, Gladys," he said. "Call Pots. Tell him to get his ambulance out here."

Mr. Norman dropped the telephone and ran past me down the ramp that overlooked town.

I took two quick steps and stopped at the top of the ramp. All of Grayson spread out in front of me, all five hundred people worth.

Mr. Norman jumped the tracks and headed for the man.

Past the train station, the Mountie's car slid sideways, threw up a cloud of gravel and dirt, and disappeared into the ditch. For a second, all I could see was his big cloud of dirt. Then his engine screamed, and he shot out of the ditch. He jumped the tracks doing about a hundred miles an hour, landed, and tore down the road with the cloud rolling behind him.

To my left, I could hear men gathering in the street. Mostly they were hollering to call Pots and the Mounties, but one was even hollering to call Dr. Wilcox.

Mr. Phillips came out of the hardware, slammed his door, and started running toward Happy Valley.

Jane Howe stuck her head out the beauty parlor window. She had curlers in her hair. She must've figured she wouldn't be much help with a head full of curlers, so she just craned her neck and watched everybody running.

Pots stood in the doorway of his insurance office. He folded his hands behind his back and looked over his nose toward Happy Valley. It seemed like forever before he pulled his door closed, locked it, checked it twice by jiggling the doorknob, and strolled up to the hardware corner, then crossed

Main Street to Gunther's gas station, where the ambulance was kept.

I ran down the ramp, turned the corner at the bottom, and headed for the tracks.

Arthur was coming from the reserve — about a hundred Indians followed him.

The Mountie's car was sitting sideways on the reserve side of Happy Valley. It was covered in dirt, and grass hung from both bumpers.

Sergeant Findley held out his arms. "Stand back, men," he ordered.

Mr. Norman kneeled and put his fingers to the man's neck.

Dr. Wilcox left his car door wide open and ran to the man. His white coat blew open, and doctor stuff made his pockets bounce up and down.

"Make room for the doctor," Mr. Norman called.

Dr. Wilcox pushed his way into the crowd.

"For God's sake, men," Mr. Norman called again. "Give the man some room."

The crowd of white people and Indians opened up to let the doctor through, then closed back around him.

Arthur ran past everybody and stopped beside me on the mound of rocks that held the railway tracks. "He's alive," Arthur said between breaths. "There's too much fuss for a dead man."

"Yeah," I said, and made a big sigh. "I think so, too." But I didn't believe it. I just said it to make Arthur feel better.

Dr. Wilcox bent over the man, and among all the legs I could see him working. He breathed air into the man, got a worried look, then hit the man on the chest as if he was trying to get the air back out.

He got another worried look, held his fingers to the man's neck, then put his ear to the man's chest. He looked up at Mr. Norman and made a quick nod.

Mr. Norman jumped. "Get a stretcher!" he called. "He's alive!"

Arthur let out a big breath.

I looked back at where the man was lying. The eye was in my head again, following me with its dead look, pestering me like it was trying to blame me for something I didn't even do.

He Said It Like a Cuss

Sergeant Findley looked down at me and Arthur. "You boys find this fella?"

Sergeant Findley had a long red mustache that hung over his mouth. Sometimes food got stuck in it. Today, a piece of strawberry jam swung from a clump of hairs right in the middle.

My head moved in time with the swinging jam.

"Well?" he asked.

"Yes, sir," Arthur said.

He looked at me. "What's wrong with your head, boy?"

The jam swung to the right.

"Can't you talk?" He wiped his mustache. Now the jam was stuck in some other hairs on the left side of his mouth. He bent over and pushed his face so close our noses almost touched. He smelled like cigarette smoke and coffee. "Maybe you've got something to hide?"

"I didn't do anything." I leaned back against the rail but he just followed me.

"How old are you? Twelve? Thirteen?"

"Almost thirteen."

"That's old enough to know how to talk."

"Yes, sir."

"Good. Don't forget it." He stood and gave us a hard look. "I've got more questions for you two, so don't try to sneak off."

He turned and went back to Dr. Wilcox and Mr. Norman. They were trying to get the hurt man into the ambulance without killing him.

Sergeant Findley held out his arms. "Men," he said to the crowd in a big voice. "There's nothing left to see."

Pots folded his arms across his chest and leaned against the ambulance. He had white hair and big ears and a long skinny body. He was giving orders, but he wasn't moving much himself. He just stood there, like he would rather go to the morgue than the hospital. I could see Pots looking around the crowd for somebody to pick on. Then he spotted me. He didn't even bother to get off the side of the ambulance or unfold his arms. He just said in a loud voice so everybody could hear, "Well, if it isn't Little Willy Yellowfly — the whitest redskin in Grayson."

A man standing next to Pots slapped his leg and laughed like he'd heard the best joke in the world.

I put my head down so the rest of the men would think he was talking to somebody else.

Arthur elbowed me. "Pots looks like *aapaiai* — a weasel in winter coat."

"He's a worse bully than Woody Loewan," I said.

"He cheats people on insurance," Arthur said.

Arthur didn't know that on his own. He knew it because I told him, and I knew it because Dad told me.

I sat on the rail and put my chin in my hands.

When Pots wasn't giving orders, he was complaining about how his back hadn't been this sore since he put old Mrs. Jones on his stretcher and slid her down a flight of stairs and out into the ambulance. And she weighed close to three hundred pounds. He said he could hold the door and drive, but somebody else would have to do the loading and unloading.

Mr. Norman and a tall Indian man grabbed hold of the stretcher.

"Okay," Dr. Wilcox said.

The men lifted and started walking.

"Careful, men. He's hurt bad," the doctor said.

The man's arms flopped around.

"Darn, I said be careful." Dr. Wilcox caught the arms, folded them across the man's chest, and held them there as they walked with the stretcher.

The hurt man was wearing an army shirt. Somebody had written "SIKSIKA" in bold letters on the shoulder. *Siksika* is what Blackfoot called themselves. But it still didn't look right. I guess I was expecting to see "CANADA" written in that spot. I wondered why I hadn't noticed it before. Maybe it had been covered in dust. Or maybe I was just too scared to see straight.

I tried to look away, but the eye caught me watching. I knew he was alive, but that eye still gave me the willies. It didn't seem to notice anyone but me. Maybe it was following me because I was the first person it saw, or maybe it was trying to get me to do something I'd regret.

Arthur had his eyes closed and his head down. He looked as if he was praying, or maybe he was just too scared to look at the eye.

"You got the willies, too?" I asked.

"I can't stand to look," he said to the ground.

"I hope Pots turns on his light and his siren."

Arthur shook his head.

I guess I should've thought of something better to say. But I couldn't think of the right thing, so I just made nervous talk. "Maybe he was in the war," I said.

Arthur stopped shaking his head and looked at me. "What war? The one against the Germans or the one right here?"

I'd given up trying to talk and had gone back to watching the hurt man disappear into the ambulance when Dr. Wilcox said, "Whoever found this Indian fellow probably saved his life."

"It was the Squat-to-Pee brothers," Pots said, and pointed at me and Arthur.

The man beside Pots was bent over holding his stomach, trying to catch his breath from laughing at Pots's joke.

I sat still, looking at the ground, feeling the heat from Arthur's shoulder on my own.

Pots was always saying I looked like an Indian because Arthur was my friend. Arthur figured I was as close to an Indian as he'd ever seen in a white kid. He even decided I looked like I could be his brother. I figured that was okay because Arthur didn't have a brother of his own. I could stand being an Indian for Arthur.

Pots slammed the big back doors of the ambulance. It was really a Fargo panel truck that was turned into an ambulance. It was painted bright white with red crosses on both sides and the back.

The red light flashed in my eyes as it made its big circle. Then the siren started to warm up. By the time the ambulance got to the road, the siren was screaming.

Arthur had finished praying or being scared or mad or whatever he was doing. I said, "Dad says that if Pots doesn't turn on the red light and the siren, the man in the back is already dead. So I guess he must be okay." I figured that was the right thing to say.

"Or maybe he's not hurt at all," Arthur said.

Arthur was hoping. I knew Arthur was feeling bad because the hurt man was an Indian, and I knew he was feeling worse than if the man was white. It's only natural to feel bad when your own kind gets hurt.

"Dad said Dr. Wilcox will doctor Indians just like they were white."

Arthur didn't say anything. He just looked at me.

I was getting ready to talk about how Dr. Wilcox was such a good doctor because he was in the war, too, and was used to doctoring soldiers who were nearly killed. But Sergeant Findley came back and stood in front of me and Arthur. His head blocked out the sun. It hardly had any hair and was shiny from sweat. The hair that was left was only a thin strip of red fuzz that went back around his head between his ears. It looked like wheat trying to grow in an alkali patch, and alkali will hardly grow weeds.

"Which way did you two come from?" he asked.

We both pointed east to my house.

"Where do you live?" he asked Arthur.

Arthur pointed west along the tracks.

Sergeant Findley motioned with his head. "In that shack a mile off?"

Arthur nodded.

"You see anything?"

Arthur shook his head.

Sergeant Findley turned his big head to me. The sun looked like it had grown ears. "What time did you find him?"

"Fifteen minutes ago."

Sergeant Findley sat on his haunches and faced us straight on. "Either of you see anything suspicious? Any Indians hanging around?"

We both shook our heads.

His arms hung loose from where they rested on his knees. They were covered with the same thick red fur that was everywhere but on his head. On the back of his hand, stuck in the hair, was the piece of jam. He turned his furry arm and looked at his watch.

"It's eleven o'clock now," he said, standing. "Can see pretty good." He looked up the tracks to the west and then down them to the east. "You would'a seen Indians if they were here."

I gave Arthur a nod that meant I agreed.

Sergeant Findley pulled his belt loops and lifted his pants. His stomach went up with the pants, then both went back to their natural position.

"I don't suppose the time matters much. If he wakes up, I expect he'll tell me what happened. But it looks pretty clear to me. He got hit by a train."

He pulled his belt loops again and walked over to his car. When he opened the door, I could see his Mountie hat sitting on the seat. He pushed it over and climbed in. I figured he would follow the ambulance. He didn't. He just sat there for a long minute, and when he did move, he backed up, right to me and Arthur, and stuck his head out the window.

"It's Yellowfly," he said, like he was cussing Arthur.

He turned the car and headed down the path and up onto the main road, following the trail of dust that hung over the road behind the ambulance.

It seemed like we stood there forever. Yellowfly. That was the worst person it could have been, a hero to Indians.

Arthur's Grandpa Called Them *Kaxtomo*

Arthur and I sat on the rail and looked out at the reserve. The road dirt hung in the air for a long time before it settled into the ditches.

"The Mounties won't catch the one who did it," Arthur said.

"Catch who? Sergeant Findley said Yellowfly got hit by a train."

"Yellowfly got beat up by a man."

"How do you know it wasn't a train?"

"A train would'a made him into a hundred pieces. We'd be sitting in pieces of him right now." Arthur looked at his feet, then back at me. "Do you see any pieces?"

"No," I said.

"That's because there was no train. I just walked down the tracks on my way to your house. I'd'a seen a train."

Arthur was right. Sergeant Findley shouldn't be looking for a train. He should be looking for a man. And I suppose it could've just as easily been an Indian as any other man — I told Arthur this.

"If the Mounties thought it was an Indian, they'd be out looking for him right now. There's nothing the Mounties like better than throwing an Indian in jail."

"Just because the Mounties don't care to look for an Indian doesn't mean one didn't do it."

"If the Mounties would rather blame a train over an Indian, then I'd say it was a pretty good clue. Besides, Yellowfly was a hero to Indians."

"Sergeant Findley will go looking for an Indian when he figures out it's not a train he's looking for."

Arthur shook his head. "Didn't you hear what I just told you?"

"Okay," I said. "Maybe once Sergeant Findley figures out it's not a train or an Indian, he'll go looking for whoever did it."

"*Whoever did it?*" Arthur said, and smirked. "Who else is left in Grayson?"

"There's lots of people."

"No, there isn't. There's only one."

"Who?"

"A white one."

"Oh, Arthur, you don't know that."

"I just heard the Mountie blame a train when there hasn't been a train in hours. I heard him use Yellowfly's name like it was only fit for cussing with. And I've seen what happens when Indians get in trouble with white people — I saw what happened with Old Man Howe last spring."

"That was different. Yellowfly hit Mr. Howe."

"Why do you always take the Mounties' side?"

"I don't *always*. Besides, you always take the other side, especially if an Indian did something wrong."

"Well, you try takin' the Indians' side then."

"I could do it easy."

"Even when the Mounties say the Indian is wrong?"

I didn't answer Arthur because I knew the Mounties usually said the Indian was somehow to blame. I also knew if I stood up for an Indian I'd be seen as standing against the Mounties.

"But Mr. Howe is rich," I said. "You can't go around hitting rich people."

"Mr. Howe is white," Arthur said.

He picked up a rock and threw it hard. It bounced in the dirt and rolled down the path. It looked like it might go all the way to the reserve.

I found a nice round rock and gave it to him.

Arthur nodded, then went on talking. "The Mounties didn't care that Howe and Albert Loewan and Pots ganged up on one man. The only thing they care about is which one is white and which one is Indian so they know who to throw in jail."

I didn't see the fight, but I knew what happened. Everybody in Grayson knew what happened. Yellow-fly came walking down the sidewalk from Frankie's store. Mr. Howe and Albert Loewan and Pots watched him from Pots's insurance business. Howe stepped out the door and stood right in front of

Yellowfly. Albert Loewan grabbed Yellowfly's arms from behind. Mr. Howe wound up to throw a good punch, but Yellowfly slid an arm loose and knocked Howe down with one punch. He pulled his other arm free and knocked Loewan down with another punch. Then Pots came tearing out of his office swinging a baseball bat like a madman. Yellowfly bobbed and weaved and hit Pots once and knocked him down.

I found a good throwing rock and rubbed it on my pant leg.

Arthur was still rolling his in his hand.

The town people said Yellowfly was tormenting them by walking around with his medal hanging where everybody could see it. At first, I agreed with them, and had even called Yellowfly a show-off. That caused nothing but trouble between me and Arthur. A few times we'd even got our fists up and danced and kicked dirt at each other and hollered, "I'll show you, white man," and, "It'll take a tougher Indian than you." It nearly wrecked our friendship.

"The Mounties threw Yellowfly in jail," Arthur said. "And the judge sent him to prison for three months." Arthur's face was red, and he was breathing in short, quick breaths.

When Yellowfly got out of jail, he'd walked around town saying, "Three men. Three punches."

"Yellowfly was wearing his war medal on his chest right where everybody could see," I said. "He did it to torment the town people, like he was better than everybody, even Mr. Howe."

"Yeah," Arthur said. "Then what happened?"

"I can't remember."

"Mr. Howe snuck up on Yellowfly and sucker punched him. Nothing happened to Howe, but Yellowfly got thrown back in jail."

Me and Arthur threw our rocks. And if they hadn't run into each other, they would've rolled all the way to the river. And the river was about ten miles from Happy Valley.

I didn't like to see anybody get sucker punched. After that, I'd even started to pull for Yellowfly a bit. I knew Arthur would feel pretty good if he heard me say that Yellowfly was the only war hero I knew. But I never told Arthur this. I guess I wasn't much of a friend.

"But Mr. Howe is rich," I said instead.

"Yeah, he's rich, but mostly he's white."

"I still think Sergeant Findley will catch the man."

That just made Arthur mad.

"You're stupid, Will Samson. The Mounties don't care about Indians and neither do the people in Grayson."

I considered what Arthur had said.

"I can't do anything for Yellowfly," I said.

"You could help me catch the man who beat him."

I'd listened to Arthur complaining about the Mounties and white people in general for so long that I was even beginning to understand why he got so mad all the time. And I guess he'd kind of just worn me down with his talk, so I said, "Okay. I'll help you catch him."

Arthur looked a little surprised, like he thought he'd have to work on me for a hundred more years just to get me to say something nice about an Indian without being paid a nickel or having dirt poured into my ears.

"I mean really catch him," Arthur said. "Not just fooling around, like it was a game."

"Sergeant Findley'll get mad."

"We won't tell him."

"Dad'll get even worse mad."

"We won't tell him either," Arthur said. "We won't tell anybody. We can't."

I stared at Arthur for a minute. His skin was the color of tanned leather. His eyes were black like they were all pupil, and his hair was black, too, and short, and it stood straight up on his head. I looked the same as Arthur except I was shorter and a little lighter in all the colors. I looked like his paler little brother. I figured I could help my brother.

"What're you lookin' at?" Arthur asked.

"I just want to remember what you look like in case this guy gets at you like he got at Yellowfly."

That turned Arthur's face back to its usual sour look.

"What kind'a man would treat a hero like dirt?" he asked.

"I don't know, Arthur."

"A *kaahtomaan*. That's who."

I shook my head. "You keep telling me Blackfoot words. Do you figure I'll just start talking like I've been an Indian all my life?"

"No. You'd have to practice."

I tried to say the word like Arthur had, but he just laughed.

"That's why I don't bother trying."

"You could say *kaxtomo*."

"Why would I want to say that?"

"They mean the same thing and it's easier to say."

"Just tell me what they mean and I'll call this dirty guy that. That'll be easier still."

"The enemy," Arthur said.

Arthur told me about when his grandpa wasn't much older than we are today, how he'd rode with Lame Bull in Montana when the Blackfeet in Montana and the Blackfoot in Alberta were still all one people — when men could still be warriors and didn't have to do what the white man's treaty told them to do. Lame Bull called the enemy *kaxtomo*. Now so did Arthur's grandpa.

"I'll give it a try when nobody's listening," I finally said.

"Why? Are you scared white people will think you're turning into an Indian?"

"Jeez, Arthur, you don't have to get mad at everything."

We didn't talk for a while. We just sat on the rail,

looking out at the reserve with Grayson behind us. We moved the rocks around with our feet and rubbed our hands on our pant legs and watched two little gophers running around acting foolish.

When I turned to Arthur, it looked like he was getting ready to say another Blackfoot word. He didn't. He just went back to talking about Mounties.

"Indians didn't trust the Mounties," Arthur said.

"Because they're *kaxtomo* ... the enemy?"

He nodded.

"I expect that's natural, the town people and the Mounties didn't trust Indians."

"How about you?" Arthur asked. "Do you trust Indians?"

"I trust you. But you're my friend — you're my *napi*."

That made Arthur smile. "You must'a been practicing that one," he said, and he handed me a nice round rock. It was about as good a throwing rock as I'd ever seen.

We sat for a while longer. Arthur talked about how Treaty Number 7 was signed in 1877, and how he'd heard stories that Colonel Macleod had tried to say *waahkoomohsi* to Chief Crowfoot — a Blackfoot word that meant a pretty big promise — but Macleod couldn't say it because the promise wasn't in his heart. Then Arthur said every white man who'd ever made a promise to an Indian had always found a way around it.

I didn't know what to think of all the stories Arthur told about Colonel Macleod. One time his own grandpa said Macleod was the only honest white man he ever knew. But Arthur wouldn't listen to that kind of talk. He'd already made up his mind about Macleod. Macleod was a Mountie. And Arthur didn't trust Mounties.

"It's hard to keep a promise to someone who isn't a friend," I said.

"And worse if you're enemies."

I told Arthur I wasn't much better than Macleod at saying Blackfoot words, and he shouldn't fault Macleod or even me if we tried and got it wrong. But I told myself I would do everything I could to keep my promise to a *napi*.

I would fight, if I had to.

A River of Steel

Arthur rubbed the dent the rail had made in his rear end and headed up the tracks for home. He hardly noticed the cloud of tiny flies hovering over the west side of Happy Valley, how they wandered up the bank of rocks and flowed around him, how the heat drifted along the polished rails like waves on water, and how he looked cloudy and dark himself as they floated together on that river of steel.

"Wait up!" I called. "I'll walk you home."

Along the way, Arthur figured out about a hundred plans to catch *Kaxtomo* — the enemy who beat up Yellowfly. But they weren't really plans. They were just a bunch of names. With every name, he would get a mean look and say, "We'll get them when it gets dark." He was doing his best to blame everybody who lived in Grayson. Once he even blamed my grandma. She'd been a pretty strong woman — when she was alive. After that, I decided to go home.

"Make your own plan then!" he called after me.

I gave him a nod and a wave and headed down the tracks for home.

I lived a mile east of town and a quarter mile north. That gave me plenty of time to think. But I wasn't working on a plan. I was just trying to forget the eye. Being alone made it worse. Every time I closed my eyes, Yellowfly's was there. And my own were getting pretty dry from not blinking enough.

I looked back the way I had come.

Sergeant Findley drove slowly past Arthur's house. He stuck his head out the window and looked into the ditch and around the yard. Then he pulled his head back inside, crossed the tracks, and turned toward town.

A cloud of dirt followed close behind his car.

I wobbled down the rail toward home. I wondered what Sergeant Findley was doing looking around Arthur's house. Maybe he didn't believe what me and Arthur had told him about Yellowfly. Maybe he was looking for an excuse to throw us in jail. All Arthur's talk about how Indians didn't trust the Mounties and how the town people and the Mounties didn't trust Indians got me thinking that I couldn't trust Sergeant Findley either.

I wobbled on a bit farther and thought about Yellowfly. I couldn't figure out why somebody would beat him so bad. I thought about Yellowfly dying. That would mean me and Arthur would be looking for a killer and not just a mean person who beat up people and left them in the dirt like they were no better than a dead gopher.

I was scared and a bit mad.

Behind me a voice called, "Hey, boy, what are you up to?"

I took off, without looking back.

"Hold up a minute, kid!" the voice hollered. I want to know what you've been doing!"

I gave a quick shoulder check. Sergeant Findley was standing by his open car door, his face red from yelling, the dirt hanging in the air like a dark cloud.

"Damn your hide if you're fooling in police business," he cussed, and slammed his door.

A Whole Bunch of Tails

I ran past the row of elevators and the long line of boxcars sitting on the west side of town. I figured Sergeant Findley would come looking for me from the town side of the tracks, so I ran down the path toward the reserve, crossed Happy Valley, and crawled behind the Saskatoon bushes.

There, I sat and caught my breath.

Happy Valley dipped just to my left. It was full of footprints where white people and Indians had trampled down the heavy dust. Only one spot had no footprints — where Yellowfly had fallen. There the footprints sat side by side with the toes pointing at the dent left by his body. It was kind of funny because it looked like the footprints were respectful of Yellowfly's shape.

I wondered what the men from Grayson would think if they knew their footprints were being respectful to an Indian. I bet they'd be mad.

The dirt path went one way to the reserve and the other way to town. I looked down it. It went beside Mr. Gunther's new cars and trucks and right on to the front door of the beer parlor.

This was the perfect spot to watch the town.

Sergeant Findley drove slowly past Gunther's gas station, turned around in the middle of Main Street, and headed back toward the beer parlor.

I figured he was looking for me.

He pulled up in front of the beer parlor and got out of his car. He stood for a second and looked at the door. Then he turned and looked right at my clump of bushes.

I ducked.

He reached through his open window and grabbed his Mountie hat, pulled it on, gave my bush a hard look, and stepped into the beer parlor. Awhile later, he came out dragging a drunk, threw him into the back seat of his car, and drove off.

I figured I was safe for as long as it took Sergeant Findley to lock up the drunk. I crawled out of my hiding place and walked into the hollow to look around. Something felt lumpy under my feet, like I was walking on popcorn. I rolled it around with my foot, knelt, and felt it. It was drops of blood mixed with the flour dirt. And where Yellowfly had fallen, where the respectful footprints were looking, was a hard piece of dark ground.

I reached in and touched it. The dirt was dried hard with blood. It felt kind of warm.

I stood and looked east to the place where me and Arthur had first seen Yellowfly. I looked west to where Arthur had come on his way to my house. Then I looked at Yellowfly's shape in the ground. He couldn't have been lying here when Arthur came walking along the railway tracks or Arthur would have seen him. Yellowfly must have walked into Happy Valley after Arthur passed.

I looked back at the bushes. They were scruffy, but they would hide somebody pretty good. A perfect place to watch from, if you were planning to beat up an Indian.

I made a quick check of town. No Sergeant Findley.

I walked back to my hiding spot behind the Saskatoon bushes and crouched down. I could see the railway tracks, the hotel with the beer parlor on the ground floor, and the path that went behind me to the reserve.

I figured *Kaxtomo* had waited here. If Yellowfly had come from the reserve, he would have seen him hiding, so Yellowfly must have come from town. And if *Kaxtomo* had been hiding when Arthur came by, then he had to be on the reserve side of the Saskatoon bushes or Arthur would have seen him.

Besides, it made sense. That's where I would hide if I was planning to ambush an Indian who came from town. And I figured *Kaxtomo* was as smart as me.

So that's where I started.

I crouched a little longer to see if someone would come along, and if I could see them through the bushes, and if they could see me hiding. I crouched till my legs went numb. Nobody came.

I stuck my feet into the grass under the bushes and rubbed the feeling back into my legs. That's when I spotted something furry peeking out from between my shoes. I held really still, just in case it was a live gopher; then I reached in, grabbed the tail, and gave it a quick jerk.

It was better than something alive. It was a whole bunch of gopher tails, tied in a circle with a string going through each tail. There must have been fifty of them. They were pretty stinky but I didn't mind. Mr. Phillips paid a cent a tail. I could stand a little smell for fifty cents.

Dad called gophers rats with furry tails. They wrecked crops with all their digging and eating. And their holes were about as dangerous as a German minefield — they could break a sheep's leg or a cow's leg or even a horse's leg like nothing.

When he was my age, Dad said, a whole colony of gophers got together and dug a giant hole right in the middle of a wagon trail. One night, he walked into the hole by accident. He'd still be down there if he hadn't had the sense to light his coal-oil lantern. Dad said he found his grandpa wandering around like he was looking for something. Dad said, "Let's walk out of here." His grandpa said, "Let's find my horse and wagon. Then we can ride out."

Most of Dad's stories were whoppers. I suppose that one was the biggest in all of Canada, but even if a fellow threw away the worst of the stretchers, there was still plenty of truth left over to understand why farmers didn't like gophers much.

Last summer, I'd even heard that farmers paid Mr. Phillips two cents a tail, and he'd turn around and pay out one cent to any kid who brought in a gopher tail. One time I tried to find out who those farmers were so I could sell the tails to them directly for two cents. But nobody knew who they were. After that I figured Mr. Phillips was buying gopher tails to give kids something to do and maybe even keep us out of trouble. Mr. Phillips said the tail was awfully good proof that the gopher wasn't going to be causing any more problems. He called it a bounty. I called it good money for a kid.

I counted the tails and pretty near had the fifty cents spent just sitting there, then I got a thought: What if the gopher tails belonged to Yellowfly? Fifty cents was a lot of money for a kid and maybe for an Indian, too.

Then I got a worse thought: the tails weren't Yellowfly's. If Yellowfly had dropped them, they would have been caught up in the branches, not half buried in the grass. They were *Kaxtomo's* tails. He'd been hiding behind the bushes and dropped them, right where I found them.

It made me kind of nervous to be sitting in his ambush spot and holding his fifty cents. And it scared me to think what he'd do if he caught me. Maybe he'd beat me like he beat Yellowfly.

I was just getting up when I heard footsteps crunching in rocks leading from the railway tracks and on into Happy Valley.

I ducked and held my breath.

Somebody was coming straight for me.

Looking through Frozen Eyes

My head was getting all dizzy from lack of air when I heard the voice.

"What are you doing, lad? Looking for evidence?"

I took a big breath and stuffed the tails into my pocket. When my head cleared, I stood up. It was okay. It was just Mr. Norman. He was coming down the edge into Happy Valley and leaning into the wisp of air that was rising out of the hollow.

"I was looking for money," I said. "Sometimes a crowd of men will drop some. If you look careful you can find it."

"You'd have better luck down here where the men were." He pulled his hand out of his pocket, bent to one knee, and dug around in the dirt as if he was looking for something. I knew he had money in his hand. Mr. Norman was always looking for an excuse to give kids money. "Well, look what I just found. A nickel." He rubbed it on his knee, then held it up. "Aw, darn, it's one of those '52s. That's too new for me. You want it?"

I was just walking down into Happy Valley when he flipped the nickel into the air. I caught it. "Thanks," I said.

Mr. Norman stood beside me, took out his hankie, and wiped his eyes. They stopped blinking long enough for him to look around at the heavy dust, then over at the respectful footprints and Yellowfly's shape.

I didn't know what Mr. Norman saw when he looked at the ground. Maybe he saw Yellowfly lying there like I did, or maybe he saw something else, like the war where men got killed every day. I thought about Yellowfly wearing the army shirt, how somebody had written "SIKSIKA" in bold letters on his shoulder, how it didn't look right to me, and how I was expecting to see "CANADA" written in that spot.

"Yellowfly had "Siksika" written on his army shirt," I said.

"That's what the Blackfoot call themselves."

"Why wasn't Canada written there? Wasn't he fighting for Canada?"

"We all have our reasons for going to war," Mr. Norman said. "Yellowfly went for his people, but I expect he went for Canada too."

"Did you fight in the war?" I asked.

"I managed to get into both wars. I was just old enough to catch the tail end of the first one and just young enough to catch the head end of the second one."

"Why did you go?"

"The first time I was young and full of adventure," Mr. Norman said. "The second time I was old and foolish."

"Were you a soldier with Yellowfly?"

He shook his head. "We were in different regiments."

"My dad didn't go," I said, looking at the ground.

"I know," he said.

"Dad said he had to run the farm and grow food for the soldiers and protect his family in case the Germans attacked Canada."

"It was a bad time for everybody. Your dad did his best."

"My grandpa went to the first war. He got the mustard gas and died in a trench. My Uncle Tom went to the second. He got killed by a machine gun on the beach at Dieppe."

"There's no good way to die," he said. "And there's no good war."

Mr. Norman lowered his head till his chin touched his chest. He could've been praying or maybe he was just looking at Yellowfly's shape. "What a mess," he said to the ground. "And that darn chaff." He wiped his eyes again. "Don't work in a grain elevator if you can avoid it."

We stood there among the footprints, looking at the depression in the heavy dust, my head full of thoughts that had no words to them.

I took a big breath and sighed. "I should be getting home."

"Yeah, me too, but it's still a shame this sort of thing happens."

Mr. Norman's pant legs fluttered in the breeze. He put his hand on my shoulder, to keep from blowing away, I expect. His hand didn't feel rough like I'd figured a man's should. It felt like it could've been my mom's.

"A fellow can see the whole town from that darn ramp." He paused and shook his head. "What a dirty business."

I nodded and repeated his last words.

"Well, got to get home to the missus, or she'll be calling the beer parlor any minute." He chuckled.

I smiled back because I knew he didn't drink at all.

"And you've got a nickel that needs spending." He winked at me, or maybe it was just a slow blink.

He was still standing in Happy Valley when I passed Mr. Gunther's new cars and trucks and turned down Main Street.

I ducked inside the gas station, plunked Mr. Norman's nickel into the Coke machine, and got one of Mr. Gunther's eye-popping green bottles of Coke. The Coke was cold and strong. The bottles were half the size of regular bottles, and the glass was green. I figured the Coke people boiled down the regular amount of Coke and then put it into the half-size bottles, and it was the strong Coke that made the glass green. Anyway, it was the best Coke in town.

I slouched in the big wooden chair and looked out Mr. Gunther's picture window. The gas pump looked like a tall man with one long, skinny, rubbery arm and a fat, round head. The chair was all shiny from years of men sitting and rubbing their own oil into the wood. I rubbed in some of my own and took a swig. My tongue went numb, and my eyes froze from the back.

When I looked out at Main Street, the whole north side, from Frankie's store to the bank, got all cloudy.

Behind me, I could hear Mr. Gunther's voice. "You know Pots is particular about the ambulance."

Somebody mumbled.

"Did you get her cleaned up good? Did you get all the blood?"

There was another mumble.

"Okay, wash up your pails and rags and go home."

A pail rattled, the side door opened, and water slopped out into the side street.

The door closed.

The pail rattled again.

I stretched my feet out on the window ledge and took another swig. The window looked like it was covered in frost. I rubbed the cold out of my eyes and crossed my legs. A man came out of the barber shop, walked past all the stores, and turned into the narrow alley between the pool hall and the beer parlor. There, he stood facing the wall. I had to look away, because I knew he was making room for beer. When he got to the beer parlor door, he looked down at his shoes and, one by one, wiped them on the back of his pants.

I pulled out the circle of gopher tails. They were soft and smooth, but they were still stinky. I wondered if *Kaxtomo* would be able to smell them if he got close enough. I decided to wrap them in some pages from the Eaton's catalog, to keep the smell down.

I had just finished counting the tails when I heard a horn honk.

The Mountie car was stopped at the gas pump. Sergeant Findley got out, rested his furry arms on the roof, and gave me a mean look.

I didn't need to lose the tails to Sergeant Findley either so I jammed them into my pocket. Then I jumped up and gulped down the Coke, went half blind from the cold, and headed back through the garage. I dropped the bottle, turned the corner by the ambulance, and hit for the side door.

I knocked the door open just as Woody Loewan stepped in.

He was carrying an empty pail.

I hit him with my shoulder and rolled him out into the street — right into the water and the blood.

"Samson, you son of a —" he cussed.

I ran past him and headed for the railway tracks. Woody cussed again.

He was in grade six with me, but you couldn't tell by looking at him. He was awfully big for a kid. And he was a bully.

"I'll get you at school!" he hollered.

He would have a while to cool off because it was only Saturday. But I knew Woody never cooled off about anything.

Who Do I Have Fighting for Me?

Mom put a big Wearever pot full of macaroni and canned tomatoes in the middle of the table. Beside it, she put a crock of margarine and two loaves of bread with a cutting knife. Everything was steaming, except the margarine. It smelled awfully good.

She looked at me, then waved her hand in front of her nose. "Phew, you stink."

I squeezed between the table and the wall and went to sit when Dad hooked my chair with his foot and pulled it away from me.

Tim pinched his nose and scrunched up his face. "I smell rotten gopher tails."

"I don't have any," I said.

Tim scooped up a macaroni with his spoon and flipped it at me. It missed my head and stuck on the wall. Tim was fourteen, so he could get away with more things than I could.

Dad filled his mouth with macaroni, then made a sweeping motion with the back of his hand like he was pushing some spilled salt across the table.

"Whud I do?" I asked.

He swallowed the lump. "Go to the irrigation ditch and wash up."

"How come Tim gets to wash at the well?"

"He's not going to poison our drinking water with whatever you've been rolling in."

"I didn't roll in nothing."

He took another spoonful and waved the back of his hand at me. Dad had an extra big spoon for eating macaroni and tomatoes. It was bigger than a regular big spoon but smaller than a shovel. He opened his mouth wide and loaded in another bushel, then scrunched up his face like Tim had done.

Mom gave me a piece of soap and a rag and pushed me to the door.

"Mom," I said. "They'll eat it all."

"I'll save you some."

Sometimes Mom would sneak me supper even if Dad said I was to go hungry. I knew she would give me her supper if Dad and Tim ate mine. I was just too lazy to go wash.

"I'll go after," I said.

"You'll go now, Stinky." She got a good hold of my shoulders and marched me through the porch.

"Mom, I can walk okay."

"It's not the walking I'm worried about."

"I'll wash."

"I know better than to trust a boy when it comes to washing."

"Boy," Dad called. "If you touch that pump, I'll tan your hide." Then he said, "Where's my tea, Mom?"

I went out the front door and stomped down the stairs. I ducked into the toolshed. There I found an old tobacco can, shook out the dried-up flakes, put the circle of tails in it, and twisted on the lid. I set the can on a rafter tie and pushed it till it stopped. I stepped back and looked up to see if I could see it. I couldn't.

On my way past the well, I stopped and rubbed my hands all over the iron pump handle.

A minute later, I was looking through soap bubbles at the tall grass and cattails that grew in the ditch. I was sure I could see Yellowfly's eye watching me. Or maybe it was *Kaxtomo's* eye, and he was coming to get his fifty gopher tails. I scooped up some water and threw it at my face, then scrambled out of the ditch.

I crossed the lane at a dead run, got to the twisted old lilac bush, and looked over my shoulder.

That was a mistake.

I plowed right into the side of the house, stumbled backward, tripped over a piece of beat-up eavestrough, and fell into the gravel.

I pulled myself up and ran to the porch. I jumped for the top step and slid through the doorway.

Dad looked up and pointed his big spoon at me. "Whud I tell you about running around like a fool?"

Tim made a face over his spoon and kept eating.

Mom pulled out my chair. "No need to hurry. There's plenty." She put a big bowl of macaroni in front of me. There were two fat tomatoes on top and two pieces of bread with extra margarine on the side.

I tried to smile.

"Oh, never mind being polite," she said. "Just eat." Then she messed up my hair, or maybe she actually neatened it a bit.

I wasn't thinking about polite talk. I wasn't thinking about anything except staying one step ahead of *Kaxtomo*. It wasn't working. I kept imagining myself running through Happy Valley and him grabbing me around the neck. He would jam his hand into my pocket and pull out the circle of tails and growl, "Where'd you get these?" and "Whud you see?" I couldn't answer with his hand around my throat.

I made a wheeze and a little cough.

"You catching cold?" Mom asked. She reached across the table and put her hand on my forehead. When she brought her hand back, she had some soap on it. She frowned, wiped the soap on her dress, and felt my head again.

"He's scared Sergeant Findley will catch him and throw him in jail with all his Indian friends," Tim said.

"I'm not scared of Mounties."

"Indians should be scared of the Mounties."

"Shut up!" Dad hollered.

Now I knew Sergeant Findley had come and talked to Mom and Dad, and Tim too, I guess. Maybe Sergeant Findley had told them that I was hanging around with Indians, and if I didn't stop, I would get in big trouble.

Mom touched my forehead again and looked at my face. I guess it was red from plowing into the house. "Jim, he's got some fever," she said.

"He's hot because he ran from the Mounties," Dad grumbled. "He won't be doing any running for a while." Dad opened his mouth extra wide to get the big spoon in. He pulled it out, swallowed hard, then pointed the spoon at me. "And he's not getting out of hoeing potatoes, either."

"I'm not catching cold. I just got a macaroni down the wrong way. That's all." I coughed as if I was clearing my throat and went back to eating like nothing was wrong.

When I looked up, Mom was praying over her food.

Dad didn't pray and Tim didn't pray, and I only prayed when no one was looking.

Mom prayed something about helping her boys stay out of trouble.

I stopped eating and bowed my head. I figured it was a good request.

Then Mom prayed about Sunday school, and how it would help my soul.

I started eating again. I didn't want to hear about Sunday school. I figured Sunday school is what got all this thinking and wondering and considering going on in my head. And I guess all Mom's praying and saying nice things about people didn't help the wondering much either. I knew Mom would ask God to help me find *Kaxtomo* and get that eye to stop pestering me if she knew I needed help, but she didn't know, and I couldn't tell her.

Darn promises.

Dad wiped his mouth with his sleeve and put his hands beside his empty bowl.

He was going to start talking about his day. But first he'd have a big burp, me and Tim would snicker, Mom would say "Jim," he'd roll a cigarette, and then he'd start talking.

He took a long drag and picked a piece of tobacco off his tongue. "I heard an Indian got beat up across from the Wheat Pool elevator." Smoke came out mixed in with his words.

Beat up? I said to myself. It sounded like the people of Grayson had figured out the truth even if Sergeant Findley couldn't.

"Pots said, 'The Indian could die if we don't get him to Calgary. But Dr. Wilcox wants to care for him at the Indian Hospital. Wilcox can listen to me or not. He might not die, but for sure he'll go blind in one eye.'"

I figured that must have been the eye that was looking at me.

Dad went on. "Pots said, 'The Indian was too badly beat up to say for sure who he was.' Said, 'His own mother wouldn't know him.'"

Dad liked to talk like that.

He made a beat-up look on his face and watched us through the smoky cloud. He kept one eye closed until the smoke cleared. Then he moved the cigarette to the other side of his mouth. Pretty soon that eye was closed and the first one was open.

"But Pots figures he's that Yellowfly fella. The same one who caused trouble with Howe last spring." Dad looked around the table for a reaction.

Tim and Mom were quiet. I guess it was news to them.

"Good," Tim said.

"Was he fighting with Mr. Howe again?" Mom asked.

Dad stopped his round-the-table look at me. "Pots said you were there."

I knew Dad expected me to side with him and Tim. I knew he wanted me to say Yellowfly had it coming, but I couldn't do it. Maybe it was getting pestered by that eye or maybe it was my promise to Arthur.

"Yeah, I was there," I said. "I saw Pots. He was complaining about his back and crying about the dirt on his ambulance." I was making up stuff as I went. "He just stood there like a loafer. He was too lazy to do the job he was getting paid for."

That was one of the things Dad always said about Pots. So Dad took it from there himself.

Mom reached over and touched my forehead again. "Maybe you're not so sick after all," she said, and grinned.

Tim was nodding and agreeing with everything Dad said.

Mom said that Pots was a bully when he was a kid and never outgrew it. "There's nothing worse than a full-grown bully," she said.

I wasn't thinking about Pots or how much of a bully he was at any time of his life. I was trying to think about nothing at all. But my mind wouldn't have anything to do with nothing thoughts. In a second, I was back in Happy Valley. Yellowfly was lying in the dirt curled away from me like when Arthur and I found him. But instead of lying still, he rolled over and looked up at me. He was a worse mess than I remembered, and the eye wasn't just staring at me, it was looking at my feet then my legs and my body and finally my eyes. When he got done checking me out, he said in a rough whisper, "You know who I am. I'm the one who got thrown in jail for defending myself against a gang. Now look at me, beat up, half killed, and for no good reason." The eye looked at the trampled flour dirt, then back at me. "And who do I have fighting for me?"

"Nobody," I whispered back. I mushed my macaroni with my spoon. I wasn't hungry anymore.

Dad went on talking about other important things that had happened today. He didn't say anything more about Yellowfly. Yellowfly was just some Indian who didn't matter any more than a dead gopher.

Dad's words and smoke floated around the room. Mom and Tim nodded at them.

I thought about Arthur. I wondered what his dad talked about at the supper table. I'd bet he was trying to figure out who beat up Yellowfly. And I'd bet Arthur didn't have to be careful — always watching so he didn't say something nice about an Indian.

I Came to See Arthur

Dad stuck his arm out the driver's-side window and slapped the door. "Not everybody in this family gets Sunday off," he called.

I climbed into the truck and sat beside him.

Mom reached through my window and adjusted my bow tie. "You little Shaker," she said.

"Mom, I'm a United, not a Shaker."

Mom was always teasing me by saying I was like something, when really I was nothing like that at all. I think she was just hoping. Anyway, Shakers were pretty religious people. I wasn't even a very good United, and anybody could be a United.

Mom dropped a nickel into my shirt pocket and gave it a pat. "This is for the collection plate, not Mr. Gunther's Coke machine."

"Good Lord, let's go," Dad said.

Mom was pointing to her own pocket and shaking her finger at me when Dad turned down the lane.

Dad was fighting with the old truck. He gave it a double clutch, and it let out a loud grinding noise from the gearbox. He jammed the shifter and cussed.

The truck backfired, nearly stalled, then took off with a roar. Dad's head jerked backward and hit the window. When he looked over at me, he had a good grip on the steering wheel and was gritting his teeth.

"You figure a Shaker could drive the devil outta this cantankerous old truck?" he asked.

"I'm a United, not a Shaker."

"And a miserable-looking one at that."

"I had a bad dream."

Dad jammed the shifter forward hard and fast and caught the old truck sleeping. Before it could complain, we were tearing down the gravel at almost thirty miles an hour. "Bad dreams," he said. "That's the only kind I get. You don't see me with a long face."

"I look stupid," I said, tugging on my bow tie.

"You won't get any argument from me on that one."

I went back into my dream like it was nighttime all over again. I was standing on the railway tracks watching Yellowfly getting put into the ambulance. The eye was looking at me, pestering me, as he reached up and pulled Mr. Norman down to his face. Mr. Norman tried to look away, but Yellowfly was too strong. When their faces were almost touching, Yellowfly made his coarse whispering sound. I could hear him okay — like it was me he was whispering to. "Will you find the man who did this?" Yellowfly said. Mr. Norman turned his head. "Promise me," Yellowfly said. Mr. Norman opened his mouth but nothing came out. "Say it," he said.

I pushed my hands over my ears and squeezed my eyes closed. "Okay, okay, I promise."

"What?" Dad hollered over the motor. "Promise what?"

"I promise I'll go to Sunday school."

"Ha. You'll never keep that one."

I stared out the window. I saw myself and my bow tie staring back at me from the fender mirror.

"Church will help get rid of your misery. But I don't know about that stupid look."

"I'm not worried about getting rid of nothing."

"That's what all sinners say."

I didn't think that church would get rid of anything today. I wasn't going to church. I was going to see Arthur, and maybe that would get rid of my misery.

Dad pulled up in front of the church and stopped. The big doors were closed and everybody was inside singing.

"I guess I'm too late," I said.

The motor chugged, backfired, then died.

Dad pushed on the starter with his foot. The motor rolled over slow and mournful. "Damn," he said, and looked at me. "Whud you say?"

"I'm too late."

"It's never too late for a sinner."

"But they've started."

"You've got a whole week's sinning to get out and only an hour to do it in," he said, pushing on the starter.

It made a ticking sound.

"Okay. But I'm going to sit in back."

I got out of the truck and stuffed my hands into my pockets. One had the circle of gopher tails. I'd got it from the toolshed and wrapped it in two layers of Eaton's paper. If I left them alone, they hardly stunk at all.

I opened the church doors and stepped into the entrance. There, I sat on the floor and leaned against the inside doors. Behind them, the people were singing about Jesus.

Outside, the mournful starter had died down to nothing, and Dad was cussing up a storm. The truck door slammed and metal rattled in the box.

I peeked through the crack where the two outside doors met. Dad had the hand crank out and was turning over the motor.

"Darn truck," I said.

I pulled my knees up and listened to another song. Church songs always sounded better when I sat, like now, or when I walked by on the street. Maybe it was because my singing was so bad that it ruined the song. Or maybe there was something in the wood, and the glass and the plaster — something in the old church itself from all those years of singing to Jesus — something that got stuck on the words and made them better just because they came from a church.

The truck motor sputtered, backfired, sputtered again, then caught. Dad let out a "Hallelujah," just as the song ended. A second later, he ground a gear. The truck complained as it pulled out onto the street.

I said a hallelujah myself and headed downtown.

The downtown started across the street from the United Church, wandered the three blocks, and ended at the Bank of Commerce.

At the hardware, I turned left, crossed Main Street on a slow angle, headed down the path between Mr. Gunther's new cars and trucks, and walked over the railway tracks.

I stopped on the edge of Happy Valley and looked at Yellowfly's shape. To my left, Sergeant Findley's car crossed the railway tracks, then turned down the road that went parallel to the CPR land.

"Oh, darn," I said.

Just on the reserve side of Happy Valley, a second path cut through the prairie grass and followed the tracks. I took it and walked fast at first, then started to run. In a few seconds I was running flat out.

Sergeant Findley drove down the road, keeping his speed the same as mine. He had his window rolled down, and he was shaking his finger at me.

Arthur's house was still a long mile away.

I ran hard.

My heart pounded in my throat.

Gophers whistled and jumped for their holes.

I got two hundred yards and fell over.

Sergeant Findley stopped.

I got up and ran another hundred yards.

Sergeant Findley was already stopped when I bent over and grabbed my knees. And when I got to Arthur's road, the Mountie car was parked at an angle half in the ditch where he'd pulled ahead of me to cut me off. The driver's door was open, and Sergeant Findley was watching me over the roof.

I turned off the path, up the ditch bank, and ran right past his car. He didn't even try to grab me. I jumped the far ditch and landed on another path that ran through the packed-dirt yard, made long stumbling steps to Arthur's house, and fell onto the door.

I leaned there for a minute and looked back toward Grayson. Sergeant Findley had turned around and was already halfway to town. Before I could knock, the door opened, and I fell backward into the shack, landing between a pair of large unlaced boots.

An old Indian man looked down at me.

I took a big breath.

"*Anistau*," he said, and held his arms out as if he was talking to the whole world. "*Ikaiayiu*."

"Huh?" I said.

"His name is *Ikaiayiu*: He Runs Fast."

It was Arthur's grandpa. He was about a hundred. He was always giving me Indian names. Last time it was Little Pale Face.

I wiped the sweat on the sleeve of my white shirt. "I don't need another name. I just need to see Arthur."

"Get up, *Ikaiayiu*," he said, as he pushed me with his foot.

He was the same size as the door. He had long gray hair that hung over his shoulders. And his face looked like an old work boot that had been left outside for its whole life.

"Poop," he said.

I stared at him. I thought he meant me — that maybe Sergeant Findley had scared more out of me than just sweat.

"Poop," he said, and pointed to the outhouse.

You Two Done Talking?

Arthur's dad built the outhouse from old boards he got to keep after he tore down the CPR snow fence. The wood was so dry that all the knots fell out before he got it home. He'd nailed the tops from tin cans over the holes, but there were still some pretty good-sized cracks between the boards. A fellow could see somebody sitting on the hole without opening the door.

Arthur's pants were piled up around his ankles and the end of his belt rested on the floor between his shoes.

I sat on the dirt path in front of the outhouse and took out the circle of gopher tails. On the Eaton's paper was a steel leg trap for fifty-nine cents.

From inside the outhouse came sounds of paper tearing, then being crunched up, then uncrunched, then crunched up again. Arthur had an Eaton's catalog. All the crunching was him making the paper soft for wiping.

I stuffed the gopher tails and the picture of the trap back into my pocket. I would show Arthur the tails after I got rid of my miserableness. I'd start by telling him my dream about Yellowfly, then maybe we could figure out why the eye was pestering me.

I put the nickel on my knee. It didn't belong to me. It didn't belong to anybody on this Earth. Mom said it belonged to God, and only God would know how to spend it.

Inside the outhouse, the catalog thumped on the floor. The door banged open, and a whoosh of stinky air rushed past me. Arthur stood, zipping up his pants and hooking his belt.

"You look funny," he said.

"I look stupid."

"Maybe a little of both." He motioned to the open door. "You wanna go?"

"No. You wanna see one of God's nickels?"

Arthur stuck out his hand.

I flipped the nickel.

It tumbled in the air and landed in his palm. "Good flip. I didn't even move."

"That's because it was guided."

"By God?"

"I guess. That makes it yours."

He said thanks to God because it was really His nickel and thanks to me because I was so generous with somebody else's money.

"I already got a nickel from Mr. Norman," I said.

"He's always giving kids money."

"I spent it on one of Mr. Gunther's green Cokes."

"Freeze your eyes?"

"All the way from the back."

Arthur's grandpa was sitting on a chopping stump. Behind him the woodpile was leaning against the house. All around were the wood chips from twenty years of splitting poplar logs. He was resting for his next chopping fit.

"I dreamed about Yellowfly," I said.

"Whud he say?"

Arthur was always interested in dreams. He said they were really visions. I believe Indians had them quite a bit. Anyway, he said they told the future.

"He said we'd better find this enemy guy, or else."

"*Kaxtomo.*"

I nodded.

"Or else what?" Arthur asked.

"He didn't say."

"Did he say who *Kaxtomo* is?"

"No, he said it was our job to find him."

We stood facing the woodpile. The old man got up and put a block of wood on the stump and split it with one clean stroke. He put the two pieces together on the woodpile and sat down again. It was hardly a chopping fit.

"That's it?" Arthur asked. "That's all he said?"

"No, he made Mr. Norman promise."

"Mr. Norman?"

The old man looked up.

I told him how Mr. Norman was in the dream and how he couldn't talk.

Arthur nodded and said it's hard to get any sound out at all in a dream.

I rubbed my chin like I was thinking. I knew it helped Dad with his thinking, but it didn't do much for me beyond getting the dirt on my hands moved up to my face, where everybody could see it.

"Maybe Mr. Norman knows a secret," Arthur said. "And that's why Yellowfly was whispering."

I told him how it felt like Yellowfly was really whispering to me and how while Dad was driving me to church I had hollered to Yellowfly, "I promise."

Arthur looked suspicious. "Maybe it's you who has a secret."

"People in Grayson are always saying things about Indians."

"That's not much of a secret."

"I know," I said. "But if you listen to them long enough, they'll turn you into one of them. They'll make you hate Indians."

"Is that your secret? You hate Indians?"

"Aw, Arthur, I'm just saying people can be pretty rough."

"You have to be rough right back."

I nodded. "Okay, but you don't have to live with them."

I thought about how Dad and Tim had said Yellowfly had the beating coming. Then I thought about how I had said mean things about Indians, too. I had lots of reasons for feeling miserable, but that was the worst one.

I tried to tell Arthur these things. But it was like I was living in a dream, and no sound would come out of me. I guess I was afraid that if Arthur knew who I was inside, he wouldn't want me as a friend.

We stood halfway between the outhouse and the woodpile and watched the old man. He was still resting.

Arthur had a sad look when he said, "Yellowfly came to you and asked you to promise. He's a hero to the kids on the reserve. He's my hero, too, but he didn't come to my dream."

I watched the old man make two more chops. When I looked back at Arthur, his sad look had changed into a miserable one. Then it came to me. I knew what the dream had meant.

I poked Arthur in the ribs. "Ha," I said. "Do you promise to help Yellowfly?"

"That's a dumb question. Of course I do."

"Does Yellowfly need a promise from you?"

"That's even a dumber question."

"Well, why would he come to you for a promise then?" I poked him again.

Arthur's miserable look went away, and he was fighting all the pokes I was giving him. And in a minute he was poking me back and saying "Ha" over and over. "I know something else," he said.

"It's probably not about dreams," I said, and poked him.

"Yellowfly's eye isn't going to pester you anymore." Arthur didn't poke me. He just said it like he knew it all along. Then he made a big laugh. "The eye was there to pester you into promising."

When I thought about it, I knew Arthur was right. The eye hadn't tormented me since my dream.

The old man was standing with the ax at his side. "You two done talking?"

Arthur nodded.

The old man looked at me.

I nodded.

"Good," he said. "Now chop wood." He handed us the ax and went into the house.

It Was Quite a Sight

Me and Arthur were lying on the ground. We had our hands folded behind our heads, and we were looking at the blue Indian sky.

I'd known Yellowfly was a war hero even before Arthur told me. Once, I even saw his medal up close. I was in Frankie's store buying a penny's worth of jawbreakers. When I walked out into the street, I plowed right into Yellowfly's chest. The medal filled my eyes. I couldn't read the words, but I didn't have to. I knew what they meant: Bravery.

Plowing into him, and not even saying I was sorry, made me feel like I was being disrespectful to a hero. Yellowfly didn't seem to mind though. He just picked me up like I was empty, turned around, and set me on the sidewalk.

I kept looking at the medal. It was quite a sight.

Of all the wars and all the men who went from Grayson to fight, I only knew one man who won a medal for bravery. An Indian. I felt sorry for the town because they didn't have a hero they figured was worth looking up to.

Arthur's elbow touched mine.

I looked at him.

"Why are you looking at me, white man?" Arthur asked.

"No look," I said.

Here we go again, I thought, with Crowfoot and Macleod and the big No-Treaty. Arthur called it that, but he was really talking about Treaty Number 7.

"What do the Indians get from the big No-Treaty?" Arthur asked.

"No land. No buffalo. Nothing," I said.

We'd played this game a hundred times before. Arthur's grandpa would just shake his head when we did it. "No use," he would say.

Arthur pointed to the big blue circle of sky. "We used to have it all to where the sky touched the land."

"No sky," I said.

"The big No-Treaty," he said. "Good treaty for the white man, bad treaty for the Indian. I think I'll sign it." He laughed as if Crowfoot and Macleod were friends and Crowfoot was just teasing. Then he picked up a lump of dried horse poop and threw it at me.

"No poop," I said.

All Macleod ever said was no this and no that. Arthur figured that Macleod must've filled the treaty with all the no-things.

I tossed the poop back at Arthur. It hit him on the shoulder and bounced into the woodpile.

He was looking for another poop when we heard a loud snort.

A minute later, a dray pulled by a pair of the sorriest-looking horses I ever saw turned onto the dirt trail, made a big turn, and rolled past so close that me and Arthur thought we might both get a fresh poop dropped right on us. Two tall Indian men sat with their feet resting on the hitch. Arthur's mom and dad sat at the back. Their legs hung over the edge, and they were dressed in nice going-to-church clothes.

"Whoa," the driver said.

Arthur's dad slid off the deck and held out his hand. Arthur's mom gave him a little smile and let him help her. Then she smiled at me and Arthur, brushed her dress flat, and walked to the house.

The driver never turned around or even moved much more than to rub his thumbs over the smooth spots on the reins where the leather had got used to his hands. The other man sat with his elbows on his knees, his hands hanging loose, staring out at the dry prairie grass.

Arthur's dad slapped the planks that made the dray's deck.

The driver snapped the reins, and the horse let out another snort.

Arthur's dad glanced down at me and Arthur sitting on the ground and leaning on our elbows. He was as big as the old man. His hair was braided, and twisted in the braid was a piece of leather. At the bottom were some red and white beads and a small feather. His hair was black like oiled coal. He wore a white shirt and a string tie. The tie was made from a thin strip of leather, held close to his neck by a buffalo head carved from bone. In his hand was a Bible.

He looked at my bow tie.

I looked at his buffalo tie.

Then he walked to the house and disappeared inside.

When I turned back to Arthur, he was staring at my bow tie like he hadn't seen it before now.

"You didn't have to get dressed up to come over and chop wood and sleep in the shade," he said.

"I snuck out of church."

"Good idea," Arthur said, like he was Crowfoot.

The door opened and the old man stuck his head out. "You done chopping?" he asked.

Arthur shook his head.

The old man looked at me.

I shook my head.

"Chop wood, then talk," he said, and closed the door.

I stood facing south toward Heavy Shield School. About halfway to the school, the dray with the two

Indian men was sitting half-hidden behind a clump of poplars. They looked like they were watching me and Arthur.

I went to ask Arthur who they were. But he had already grabbed the ax and was trying to get a piece of wood to stand still while he chopped it.

I looked back at the men. I decided to call the driver Watcher and the other man His Brother.

I Decided to Use Sneakiness

Arthur chopped and I stacked. After half an hour, we switched. We were in the middle of a big rest — leaning back-to-back and as close to sleeping as I'd been since I woke up this morning — when Arthur's mom came out. She had two tin cups, a tall tomato juice can all steaming with tea, a bag with sugar, a can of evaporated milk and bannock that had been cooked on a stick and the hole filled with strawberry jam.

I perked up in a hurry when I smelled the bannock.

Arthur tipped the chopping stump, and the wood chips fell off.

His mom put the bannock in our hands and the tea on the stump.

Arthur said something in Indian. I think it was thank you. We were licking jam off our fingers and drinking tea before she got back to the house.

Arthur took out the nickel I'd given him and polished it on his pants, then he held it up and turned it. The sun caught the beaver's body and shone back into Arthur's eyes.

"Thanks," he said.

"I've got something else." I pulled out the two layers of Eaton's paper, unwrapped them, and put the tails on the stump.

Arthur's eyes bugged out. "Wow," he said, and started counting.

"There's fifty."

"Wow, fifty cents." He rubbed his nickel harder.

"It's more than that."

"Can't be better than fifty cents."

"Yes it can," I said, grinning. "It's a clue to who beat up Yellowfly."

I told Arthur how I had found the tails. And I told him how they were lying on the ground in a way that pointed to somebody hiding in the bushes. I said it must have been *Kaxtomo*.

Arthur nodded as a sign that he agreed, but his mouth was still open a little from me being right about the tails being worth more than just money. When he finally closed his mouth, he said he knew Yellowfly didn't hunt gophers, so Yellowfly couldn't have dropped them.

I told him how I had hidden in the Saskatoon bushes and watched the town like *Kaxtomo* had. I said maybe *Kaxtomo* had been waiting there when Arthur came by on his way to my house.

"But who is he?" he asked.

"I don't know."

"Somebody pretty mean."

"Even I know that," I said.

Arthur took a drink of tea and rubbed his chin. When that didn't drag out any ideas, he bent down, picked up a sliver of wood, and picked his teeth. A stuck strawberry seed can make figuring awfully tough.

"Maybe it was Howe," he said, and looked at the seed.

I laughed. "Mr. Howe is rich. He wouldn't hide in the bushes. He would hit a man right on Main Street. And let the Mounties haul the man to jail."

"Maybe somebody who works for Howe," Arthur said. "Somebody who also hunts gophers."

He picked up another sliver and gave it to me.

I picked my teeth and considered what Arthur had said. I thought about how Dad had said Mr. Phillips is the only person for thirty miles who buys gopher tails. And how it's kids he buys them from. I told Arthur this.

"Kids beat up Yellowfly?" Arthur shook his head like he couldn't believe it. "It would take ten or twenty. Yellowfly was a soldier. He fought Germans. He got a medal."

"I never heard of anyone but kids hunting gophers."

I went to talk, but Arthur held up his hand. Then he looked at the tails lying on the stump. He leaned back and thought. He made them into a circle.

The circle was the size of a ball cap.

He got up, walked over to the woodpile, and scratched his head. He came back and felt where the string went through each tail. He pulled on the string and checked the knots. Then he leaned forward as if he was going to smell them.

I bent over the stump, gave the tails a good sniff, and made a sour face. "Sure stinky. Figure that's a clue?"

He motioned for me to be quiet, thought for a while longer, then said, "It's a good clue."

"Because they're stinky?" I asked. "What does it mean?"

"It means they came from gophers."

"That's all?"

"And you shouldn't carry them around in your pocket."

"Okay, they stink," I said. "So what makes them a good clue?"

"They came from Phillips's hardware."

I went to sniff them again, but Arthur stopped me.

"You can't smell the hardware," Arthur said. "But you can figure it out."

"How?" I asked.

"First, they didn't come from kids because kids can't hang on to more than five or six, let alone fifty, before they have to run to the hardware and turn them in for money."

"And buy one of Mr. Gunther's green Cokes," I said.

"Or jawbreakers at Frankie's store."

Arthur was right. I did it and he did it and every kid in Grayson did it. I was getting ready to talk about the last time we snared a bunch of gophers, but Arthur held up his hand again.

"Second," he said. "They came from the hardware. If you needed fifty gopher tails in a hurry, where would you go?"

"The hardware," I said.

Arthur held up his hand, and I wasn't even going to talk. "Look, they're special," he said, showing me the tails. "They're tied nice and strong with a space between each tail and a good knot to hold them there."

I watched and listened. It looked like all the chin rubbing and tooth picking and walking around was going to make an idea.

He pointed out that the string didn't go through the base of each tail, it went through about an inch above the base, like they were made to stand up, like they were made to go around something. Then he pulled up one knee like he was getting ready to hug it. He took the tails and slid them over his knee.

I looked at them. They made a nice circle and stood up tall and straight.

"*Kaxtomo* made them," I said.

"And Mr. Phillips knows who he is."

"I'm going right now to ask him," I said, and got up.

"Don't be stupid. He'll tell the Mounties."

"Okay, I'll ask Sammy Phillips."

Arthur shook his head. "He'll tell his dad, and his dad will tell the Mounties."

I sat down and waited.

"Isn't Sammy in grade six with you?"

"Yeah, why?"

"You could find out what Sammy knows in a way that won't make him suspicious."

"But Sammy's not my friend," I said.

"You could make him your friend."

It was kind of a mean thing to do — trying to make a friend just to get something from him. But I couldn't see any other way, so I agreed. "I guess so."

"And when you find out who *Kaxtomo* is —"

"I could come tell you," I interrupted.

"You'll have to do it by four o'clock. That's when I go back to Heavy Shield School."

"I can't find out by then."

"I know."

"I could sneak over to the school later."

"Okay," Arthur said.

Then Arthur's mom came back and took our cups and the bag of sugar and what was left of the canned milk.

I tried my best to say thank you in Indian.

Arthur gave me a funny look.

Arthur's mom looked at me for a second, then smiled and said something in Indian. I figured it meant you're welcome. She was smiling and shaking her head when she walked back into the house. I guess I'd got it wrong, but she still liked us being polite. I decided I would try being polite to my mom.

I turned away from the house and saw Heavy Shield Residential School sitting on a short hill facing east. I'd thought it looked more like a big brick fort than a school. Arthur said if you were an Indian you'd think it was closer to a jail. He said the supervisors watched the kids as if they were prisoners. They counted them all the time and got really mad if anyone tried to sneak off. It seemed like an awfully mean place.

When I looked back at Arthur, he was watching me. "Now what?" he asked.

"I don't understand why you have to stay there all week long. You live so close. Why can't you come home except on weekends?" I asked. "I don't have to stay in my school all night and all the next day and all that week and maybe the next one, too."

"How many times did I tell you?" Arthur said. "It's because I'm an Indian."

"About a hundred times," I said. "I know you have to go. And I know if you don't they'll come and drag you there. I just don't understand why."

Arthur sat on the stump and looked down at me. He took a big breath before he started to talk. "July and August are coming."

"I know."

Arthur gave me a look. "If your dad said you could come to my house anytime, what would you do?"

"I expect I would bring a blanket and maybe some spare underwear and stay all summer."

"And by the end of the summer you'd be an Indian?"

"No, I'd still be white."

"How many summers would it take to turn you into an Indian?"

"Maybe a hundred," I said.

"And how many would it take if you got to go home at night and every weekend?"

"Maybe a thousand."

"Well," Arthur said.

"Well what?"

Arthur raised his hands and slapped them down on his knees. "Heavy Shield School is supposed to turn Indians into white men. They want to get it done before a thousand years goes by."

"Oh," I said.

Arthur shook his head like he thought I was the dumbest kid he'd ever seen. That didn't bother me much, because Arthur was right. I wasn't very good at figuring out Indians, and I was even worse at figuring out supervisors and teachers and anybody at a residential school.

Once Arthur got finished shaking his head, I said I would try to sneak over to Heavy Shield School some time after my school was done on Monday. But if I couldn't find out anything by then, or if I got beat up or thrown in jail, then I would come on Tuesday. Arthur said Heavy Shield kids had to work outside in the afternoons, so that would make it easier to find him — at least I wouldn't have to stumble along narrow hallways, up and down dark staircases, and in and out of a hundred different rooms. He couldn't say where he'd be working, because the supervisors liked to give the kids who caused the most trouble the dirtiest jobs. I'd just have to snoop around till I found him.

I stood up. "I've got to get home before Dad comes looking for me."

Arthur looked at me from his stump. "Your dad will come and drag you back?" He smirked.

"What's that for?"

"They're doing it to you, too."

"Doing what?"

"They won't let you do nothing except what they say."

"Who won't?"

"White men."

Arthur was always getting mad at the white man for something or other.

"Okay," I said. "But I still gotta go."

Arthur held up his hand to stop me. "If the Mounties hear that me and you are sneaking around trying to figure out this mystery, they'll stop us, and *Kaxtomo* will get away."

"I won't say a word to nobody."

"Not even your dad," Arthur said.

I waved at Arthur and headed home.

Along the way, I thought about Sergeant Findley. If it was Mr. Norman who had got beat up, Sergeant Findley would have found the clue without any help from me. I guess Arthur was right. The Mounties won't put an Indian beater in jail anyway, so why would they need a clue?

I thought again about asking Mr. Phillips some roundabout questions about fifty gopher tails tied in a circle. It seemed like the easiest way. But Mr. Phillips wasn't stupid. For sure, he would want to know why I was snooping in his business. And in time, he would figure out that I had a clue to who beat up Yellowfly. Then he would have to tell Sergeant Findley. And *Kaxtomo* would get away. I also knew Sammy would do the same as his dad. It was only natural.

It seemed like I couldn't trust anybody.

Arthur was right — I would have to find another way to get to Sammy.

I decided to use sneakiness.

I'd Involved Him
in a Lie

I was trying to sneak out of the toolshed after hiding the circle of tails in the tobacco can when Dad hollered, "Get in here!"

I jumped and spun around.

Dad looked down at me from the half-open kitchen window and gave me the come-here sign with his finger. "Whud I tell you?"

When I got inside, he was standing by the stove. He had a cigarette in one hand and his belt in the other.

"Where the blazes were you?" he asked.

"I stayed after church," I said, watching his belt.

"For three hours?"

"I was praying."

"If that's a lie, I'll tan your hide."

I thought about Mom calling me her little Shaker. "Jesus came into my heart," I said.

"Jesus?" he said.

"I even fell on the floor once. I didn't jump around or talk a funny language, but I sure did lots of praying."

"Talk a funny language?"

He didn't know what to say, especially with Jesus helping me with a lie. I figured a big lie would work better than a little one. And if it would keep Dad from swinging his belt, that would be good, too. Besides, Dad never came to pick me up after church. He didn't even care much for dropping me off. So I figured it was a good bet he hadn't gone inside to see if I was really praying.

He smirked like he figured I was lying, but he didn't want to take any chances with Jesus. "We'll see if Jesus can help you with those two acres of potatoes."

I stared at him through the smoke.

He stared back at me, then shook his head. "Praying?"

"Lots."

"Oh, go hoe your potatoes."

As I walked down the stairs, I thought about the potatoes. When they needed work, they were mine. After they were in the root cellar, they were Dad's.

Behind me, Mom and Dad were talking.

"I can't strap him for praying," Dad said.

"I know," Mom said.

"I could strap him for lying."

"He's been acting kind'a funny since Yellowfly got beat up. Maybe he *was* praying."

"For an Indian?" Dad asked.

"No, just general praying."

"Don't let me catch him praying for an Indian. Or it'll be the strap."

"You know he prays sometimes. He got it from me."

"He's still lying."

"He can hoe potatoes for an extra hour."

"He can go without supper, too. And next time it'll be an extra hour of strapping."

If Mom said anything, I missed it.

I found my hoe right where I had left it — leaning against the fence at the potato patch. I took off my shoes, rolled up my pants, and started hoeing. At about seven o'clock Dad went to town. A few minutes later, Mom brought me my supper. It was cut-up potatoes with cut-up onions and cut-up baloney, all fried together in the same pan.

It smelled awfully good.

She set the plate on the ground where the grass was trampled flat and stood there looking at me.

I lifted a weed with my hoe and stared at my supper.

"Eat first," she said. "It's good'n hot."

I sat on the flat grass and started eating.

Mom sat beside me and leaned against the garden fence. "Fried baloney is pretty good," she said.

"Uh-huh."

She reached over my plate and made like she was going to snatch a nice big piece of baloney.

I made like I was going to poke her with my fork.

She pulled her hand back, slid her knees up, and wrapped her arms around them. She looked out over the garden. "Aren't you going to pray before you eat?"

"I already did," I said around a mouthful. "I prayed you'd bring me some supper."

She smiled at the garden.

I kept eating until everything was gone except the big piece of baloney, then I held out the plate for Mom.

She took the baloney and ate it in little bites. "Were you at Arthur's house?"

"I went after church. It was just for a while."

"You mean, instead of church. And for quite a while."

"Yeah," I said.

"How's Arthur doing?"

"He's mad. He thinks nobody cares about a beat-up Indian."

"You care about Yellowfly."

"A little, I guess."

"Did you tell Arthur?"

"No, not really."

"If he's truly a friend, you'd tell him."

"Mom," I said.

"Well, that's how it works. I didn't make up the rules. I just follow them."

"Maybe tomorrow."

Mom gazed out at my potatoes. "Arthur looks up to Yellowfly," she said after a while. "It's natural for a boy to respect a man like that."

"He was a hero in the war."

Mom turned to me and put her hand on my knee. "Your dad would've been a good soldier. He could've been a hero if he was given a chance to fight. He wanted to go, you know." She swallowed the last bite of baloney, got up, and took my plate. "Did you pray for Yellowfly?"

"Not yet."

"Well, don't forget," she said, and headed to the house.

I was going to say thanks for supper, but Mom was already up the steps and inside. I went back to hoeing. In a while, I was thinking about Mom and all her praying. I wasn't really much of a prayer. I said the odd one when I figured it couldn't hurt, but I was more of a prayer than Dad or Tim. I guess in most ways I was more like Mom.

I hoed and hoed, and at ten-thirty I stopped and looked at my work. Then I leaned on my hoe with my potatoes all around, and together we watched the sun go down. The sky turned so red it looked like the mountains were on fire. As the red died down to nearly nothing, I thanked Jesus for helping me, and I said I was sorry that I'd involved Him in a lie. And I asked, if He wasn't busy, if maybe He could watch out for me, and help me, and see that I said good words about Indians and had good thoughts about people in general. Then I said a little prayer for Yellowfly.

I leaned the hoe against the fence and headed up the lane to the irrigation ditch. I washed off the sweat and the dirt and went in for bed.

Mom was in the kitchen making bread for our breakfast.

I made a big sniff and a long drawn-out "AHH. You make the best bread of any mom I know."

"Who said that? Can't be one of my kids." She looked at me. She had dough on her hands and flour on her apron. "Good Lord, it's a stranger. Somebody call the Mounties."

"Yeah," I said. "And supper was pretty good, too."

"Go on, get to bed," she said, shooing me away. "All that potato hoeing has got you talking funny."

I dragged myself to bed. Maybe when Mom was washing clothes, I would tell her she was a pretty good washer. I'd give it another try tomorrow.

The Most Perfect Seat

Monday was the first day of the last week of school.
Mr. Parks said it like that, so all the kids wouldn't get
scared about report cards coming. He was always
saying things to make kids feel good.

Mr. Parks looked at the class. "Who can define
the scientific method?"

Nobody answered.

Sammy looked at me and motioned for me to
answer.

I slowly put up my hand.

"Mr. Samson."

"The scientific method is a way of thinking about
problems and solving them," I said.

The kids all booed.

"Okay, that's enough," Mr. Parks said.

I had the answer memorized. So did the whole
class. Every Monday of every week, Mr. Parks asked
the same question. It was just my turn.

I stood up and bowed to the class.

"Sit down, Samson!" Woody hollered.

"Class," Mr. Parks said.

Everybody went quiet.

I thought about the first Monday of the first week of school. Mr. Parks'd said it was okay for the class to experiment with where we wanted to sit. But after the first week we had to stay put, or he wouldn't be able to remember our names, and he might fail some of us just by mistake.

Mary Romano sat up front because she was nearly blind.

Freddie Cooper sat near the door because his bladder was too small. He couldn't run all the way across the classroom and then all the way down the hall and still make the boys' room with dry pants.

Sammy Phillips was the only kid who didn't get to pick his own seat. He wandered around for a while, but, because of the smell, no one wanted to be anywhere near him. So Mr. Parks sat him in the back, closest to the one window that would open. Mr. Parks said it was because Sammy had trouble staying awake and the fresh air might help. We all knew it was because Sammy smelled bad.

He smelled worse in the spring and summer when there were lots of gopher to snare and his dad was busy buying tails. When fall and winter came and there were about as many gophers as there were hairs on Sergeant Findley's head, Woody Loewan would remind all the kids how Sammy still stunk if you got close enough or were down wind. He'd even look at

Sammy, pinch his nose, start coughing and choking, turn a blue color and act like he was dying. It was then that I figured out Woody had more to do with Sammy smelling bad than Sammy did.

When it came to picking his seat, Woody didn't care where he sat, as long as it was close to Sammy, so he could torment him.

My seat was the most perfect seat. I found it through the scientific method. It took some work. I had one thing in mind — to find a seat that Mr. Parks would never look at and so would never ask a question of the kid sitting in it. First I sat in the back and crouched down nice and low. Mr. Parks asked me more questions than if I'd sat in his chair. The next day, I moved up front beside Mary. I even sat up straight and paid attention, like five years of teachers had already told me a thousand times. Mr. Parks didn't ask me as many questions, but still there was too many.

I said good-bye to Mary.

"Is that you, Will Samson?" she asked.

I moved to the center row in the middle of the class and sat up. It was the best seat so far. Mr. Parks still asked some questions, but it was bearable. So I tried crouching down. The questions went up. I sat up. The number of questions went down. Then I moved over a row to my right and tried that for a while. Then I moved two rows to the left, near the windows. That turned out to be the best. So there I was, sitting straight up in the middle of the class in the row just left of center.

When the next Monday came, I was sitting in my never-move-again-or-risk-failing seat.

Mr. Parks asked me the first question. "Mr. Galileo," he said, looking at me.

Mr. Galileo was really Galileo Galilei. Mr. Parks called him the father of modern experimentation and gave him lots of credit for the scientific method. But I think, mostly, he was Mr. Parks's hero.

"Who, me?" I asked.

"Yes, you," he said. "Please, with all your experience, could you explain the scientific method to the rest of the class."

My brain froze.

"Well?" he asked.

I thought about how rotten my seat had turned out to be.

Then Mr. Parks said, like it was a hint, "Maybe you should consider your choice of seats."

I thought again. The frost seemed to melt a little. Then it was gone completely. "First you have to make a hypothesis."

He was silent.

"Then you make an experiment to see if it is going to work."

More silence.

I got a little frosty. Mr. Parks only gave one hint, then you were on your own.

All the kids were looking at me.

Then I remembered. "You make a conclusion," I said, like it was all one word.

"Do you have one, Mr. Galileo?" he asked.

"Yes," I said.

"And what is it?"

"I think I have the most perfect seat in the class."

"I think you might be correct, Mr. Samson."

I found out later that I missed a few steps. But he didn't point that out in front of the whole class. From then on, I knew I liked Mr. Parks.

Now it was my last week in grade six and my last week in Mr. Parks's class.

He looked at us from his spot in front of his desk. "Class," he said. "Today we'll review arithmetic and science. And tomorrow we'll review reading, writing and spelling."

He made Monday and Tuesday review days, so the kids who didn't study had a chance to pass. I was one of them.

Then he said, "You will have your tests on Wednesday. And remember, you have to pass all your tests to pass grade six."

Everybody was paying attention, even Woody.

"And Thursday is the best day of all." He smiled his nice smile. "It's report card day."

It was the best day for teachers, I thought. But it was a miserable day for kids. And to do it on the last day of school seemed like a mean trick to me.

Hearing Mr. Parks talk about tests made me wonder if Arthur had to pass grade six or he wouldn't become a white man. Arthur had said the residential schools were trying to make Indians into white men. They started by making them either Anglicans or Catholics. In a second, I was sitting in Arthur's class at Heavy Shield School. All the kids were crouching down or had their books up in front of their faces or had the lids lifted on their desks. And the teacher was shouting, "You dumb kids will never go home again. You will never amount to a hill of beans if you don't learn the white man's way." Arthur's face looked awfully pale, as if the more scared he got, the closer to being white he got. When I looked away from Arthur, I saw Crowfoot sitting in a little-kid seat right up front. The teacher pulled out the big No-Treaty and started reading. "No wandering. No dancing. No singing. No language. No spirits." Crowfoot looked at the teacher. "No freedom. No life. No use," he said. "No talking," the teacher said.

I tried to get rid of the image by shaking my head. I suppose it would've worked if Woody hadn't seen me.

"Hey, Samson!" Woody hollered. "I hear somebody shaking a bag of marbles."

"I'll shake your marbles," I said back to him.

"You couldn't shake Sammy's, and even a girl can do that." He gave Sammy's shoulder a shove. "Isn't that right, girlie?"

"Yeah," Sammy said to nobody at all.

"That's enough," Mr. Parks called.

By the time Monday was finished, I was full of arithmetic. Fractions were floating around in the water inside my eyes. I divided the class into its lowest common denominator and headed outside. A group of six boys were hanging all over four girls. I simplified them into three-over-two.

Science wasn't in my head like arithmetic was. I guess it was because I didn't have to worry about science. I'd paid attention all year. Now I didn't even have to review. I liked science. That helped a bit.

I headed past the three-over-two group of kids. I was watching for Woody — waiting for him to ambush me for knocking him down outside Gunther's gas station on Saturday — when two girls turned off the sidewalk and headed for the group.

"Don't do it," I called.

They did it anyway. They joined the three-over-two group.

"One!" I hollered.

They all looked at me like I was crazy.

I went back to checking for Woody. I couldn't find him, so I tried to put him out of my head. I had more important things to do than waste my time being scared of some bully.

I followed Sammy instead.

Mary Likes You

Sammy walked with his hands pushed deep into his pockets. He checked behind a big old poplar, around the corner of our school's storage shed, and over his shoulder. Sammy did a second shoulder check and saw me.

I was running to catch up to him.

He went to run.

"Sammy!" I called, and waved.

He was looking right at me, but his body was still going forward. Then he saw it was me, and not Woody. He waved with the back of his hand.

"Hi, Will," he said.

I had one question for Sammy: Who got fifty gopher tails from your dad? That was easy. The hard part was asking it in a way that wouldn't make him suspicious.

"I'm going to your dad's store to sell some gopher tails," I said. "Maybe we can walk together. If you're going that way."

He smiled like I'd told him that Woody'd got run over by a train. He even offered to keep a step or two behind me, so if anybody jumped us they would get him first. Then he made one of his shoulder checks. His head was sure loose.

"We could walk the regular way and take our chances equally," I said.

We got as far as Mary's house and stopped. It was a tall, skinny house covered with gray siding that looked like fake bricks. Under a second-floor window, a piece of the gray stuff had fallen off and a lump of tar paper hung out like dirty underwear. It was a poor person's house — half hidden in the shadow of the Grayson water tower.

Sammy gazed at the window.

I looked at my feet for a while and tried to think of a roundabout gopher-tail question. I wasn't having much luck.

Sammy laid his hand over his heart and sighed. "Mary's the prettiest girl in the whole school," he said.

I stood quiet and respectful for a while. I even sighed once or twice myself. Then I said in a low voice, like a thought had just wandered into my head, "I've been saving up my gopher-tail money for the Calgary Stampede. You ever hunt gophers so you can get some extra money?"

He looked away from Mary's window. His eyes were all gushy. Sammy was okay. I even liked him a little, but we weren't friends. Sometimes I'd tease him for smelling bad. But mostly I'd let him be. I understood some of what Sammy was living with. Maybe he did something to Woody. But he probably didn't, because people don't need a reason to be mean. Like I figured Yellowfly got beat up for no reason.

Sammy was still holding his hand over his heart when he said, "Huh? Hunt gophers? Me? I can't go hunting gophers. I've got to work in my dad's store."

"I don't mean today. I mean anytime."

Sammy's gushy look faded into a frown.

"Me and Arthur caught twenty-two in one day," I said. "We were going for fifty, but we ran out of day. You ever hear of someone catching fifty in one day?"

"No."

"Who brought in the most gopher tails ever? That you can remember?"

"You and Arthur. Why do you care about how many somebody else is selling?"

"I was just wondering. Fifty is a lot of gopher tails."

"You sure ask some stupid questions."

"Fifty is a lot to bring at once, is all."

Sammy looked right at me. His face was a little red considering he wasn't scared. "Nobody." He stomped his foot. "Ever." He stomped it again. "Brought in fifty gopher tails."

"Okay, I was just curious."

"Jeez," Sammy said.

I guess my sneakiness was more of a pestering. But it was working okay. I found out nobody, ever in this century, kid or man, ever brought fifty gopher tails to sell. But I found out something else: Sammy didn't like me asking a lot of gopher-tail questions. I'd bet a nickel he was hiding something.

Before I could ask another question, Sammy said, "I've got to get to work." He turned and walked quickly down the street.

I was half puffing when I caught up. "Boy, helping your dad with the buying and selling of gopher tails sounds like hard work."

Sammy stopped suddenly.

I banged into the back of his head.

He turned quickly and glared at me.

I was holding my nose between my hands and wiggling it from side to side. It wasn't broken but it sure hurt.

"Who said I was selling gopher tails?" Sammy asked.

"I was just talking. I figured your dad has to get his money back somehow. I didn't mean you were selling."

"Well, he's not worried about getting his money," Sammy said. "It's my business now. Dad gave it to me."

I thought about the last time I sold gopher tails to Mr. Phillips. Sammy bought them. By now my eyes were running from the bang on my nose. I must have looked like I was crying about the sad state of the gopher-tail business.

"I can just see Mr. Howe coming in and buying a bunch of tails, making them into a nice circle, and hanging them over his fireplace like a trophy," I said.

"What would Mr. Howe want with gopher tails?"

"Maybe it was Albert Loewan then."

"Loewan?" Sammy said.

"Sure, going to buy stinky old gopher tails is more of a foreman's job."

"You're awfully nosy about someone else's business."

"I was just wondering where the tails go when the gophers don't need them and when your dad doesn't need them and when you don't need them either."

Sammy started walking again. He looked over his shoulder. "I can do whatever I like. Nobody can stop me. And you can just go home because I'm not telling you anything."

I hollered after Sammy, "I bet you'd tell Woody!" That was a mistake.

Sammy froze and turned back into the old Sammy — the one who was trying to get through another day without getting beat up by Woody Loewan.

He shrugged. "Dad will be mad if I'm late." He stood there staring, like he was waiting for permission to go.

"Oh, go do your secret business," I said.

Sammy jammed his hands into his pockets and shuffled down Grierson Street toward Main.

I stayed back a few steps, kicking myself for forcing Sammy, for not letting it come out on its own, for wrecking my best chance to solve the mystery.

Sammy snuck up on a fat poplar, gave it a quick check, then shuffled on.

My eyes were still full of water, and my nose was plugged. But I wasn't about to let Sammy off so easily. He knew something. He would tell me if we were friends, if he trusted me.

Sammy was looking suspiciously at a crooked shadow that looked like a club.

I was walking along with my head down when I heard a scream then a shout. "Samson, you son of a —"

I turned just in time to see Woody come charging out from behind the poplar with the crooked shadow. He slammed into me with his shoulder. It felt like a truck.

I let out an "Oof" and fell backward into the gravel street.

He wound up and kicked me in the rear end.

"Ouch," I said, rolling away. "Wasn't getting all roughed up with rocks enough?"

"You're lucky I'm busy or you'd get a double dose." He kicked some gravel at me and took off after Sammy.

I rolled over and spit out dirt. I sat in the road and pushed a flap of skin back in place over my elbow. Three trees down, Woody had Sammy pinned. Sammy put his hands in his pockets. It looked like he was going to give Woody something, then Woody gave Sammy a shake and took off down the street to

Frankie's store. Sammy was still leaning against the tree like he was relaxing. I guess Sammy got out of that one pretty easy.

Then Sammy came back and stared at me. Maybe he was curious to see what he usually looked like when Woody got mad.

"I thought you were going to walk behind me," I said, rubbing my elbow. "You know, so you'd get jumped first."

"I changed my mind."

"Did you give Woody something so he wouldn't beat you up?"

"No, you did," he said.

"What did I give him?"

"You gave him an excuse to beat up somebody else for a change."

Sammy looked happy. I guess me getting roughed up made him feel good. Maybe he forgot all about my stupid questions. I hadn't. I had plenty more.

We started down the street again. We were just in front of Frankie's store when I got the idea. I knew how to make Sammy my friend.

"I was talking to Mary today," I said, easy, like it didn't matter.

Sammy's head turned slowly.

"She said she likes you."

We stopped outside Frankie's big front window. Woody was inside stuffing washers into the jaw-breaker machine and filling his pockets with his loot.

Sammy turned white, then red, and his lower lip began to twitch. "Mary?" he said.

"Yeah." I shrugged. "She likes you." I started to walk away.

Sammy grabbed my arm and jerked me back. "Mary said that? About me?"

"Yeah, but she's too shy to tell you. I know Mary pretty good. She tells me stuff."

"What can I do?" Now he was shaking.

"Well, you can't just go up to her and say, 'I hear you like me.' That would wreck it. But don't worry. I can help you. You're my friend."

Sammy's eyes were all gushy again.

Yup, I'm something, I thought. A liar, not a friend. I felt a little sick. But that didn't stop me. I put my arm around Sammy's shoulder, and together we walked up the street to his dad's store. I gave him a friendly shake, like I had no shame at all. His shoulder felt warm and a little wet from sweat, not cold like I'd expected.

We walked past Cooper's machine shop, then crossed the open space that was Mr. Cooper's yard, where Dad worked putting together farm machinery. I was just warming up to ask a bunch of sneaky questions when somebody hollered.

"Hey, aren't you supposed to be hoeing potatoes?"

It was Dad.

Show Me You're a Hero

Dad stood in the middle of Mr. Cooper's machinery yard. When Dad wasn't working his own quarter section, he put together farm machinery for Mr. Cooper.

I still had my arm around Sammy's shoulder.

"Mary is the prettiest girl in the whole town," Sammy whispered.

Dad looked at Sammy, at me, then at my hand.

I pulled it down and stuffed it into my pocket.

"Why aren't you hoeing?" Dad asked.

"I just came to sell some gopher tails."

"Your potatoes come before gopher tails."

"But Mom said I stink."

"Your potatoes won't mind a little stink." He grabbed hold of a long, straight piece of steel, lifted it, and glared at Sammy. "Go home, boy." Then he looked at me and gave his head a jerk. "Give me a hand over here."

When I got to Dad, Sammy was still standing on the sidewalk. His mouth was open a bit and he had a general gushy look. I figured he was going to say Mary was the prettiest girl in the whole province.

Dad gave Sammy a hard look. "Go home!" he hollered.

Sammy jumped, ran past me and Dad, over piles of parts, and headed up the alley to the hardware.

Dad swatted me on the back of the head with his hat. "Whud I tell you?"

I bent over and lifted the other end of Dad's steel.

Woody stuck his head around the corner of Mr. Cooper's shop, grabbed one of Dad's swather parts, and took off up the street.

"Damn his hide," Dad said.

I stood there with my mouth open.

"What are you gawkin' at?" Dad said. "Go get it back. And while you're at it, kick his ass."

I ran between the piles of metal. I figured Woody was either after Sammy or he was hiding in front of Pots's insurance to ambush me. So when I got to the street, I had my arms up to protect my head, and I was shouting, "I gotta nickel for you!"

I turned the corner and stopped. No Woody. Good thing. I was fresh out of nickels.

I put my arms down and looked through Pots's open door. The whole building was no bigger than Dad's toolshed. On the wall was a bunch of insurance pictures of crashed cars and burned-down houses and crying kids and sad moms. Under the pictures it said, "Don't let this happen to you," and "Grayson Insurance can protect your family."

Pots was sitting behind his desk. A pair of half-glasses rested on the end of his nose. He was staring at Mr. Norman like a weasel considering a chicken.

"I don't know," Mr. Norman said, rubbing his neck. "It's kind of expensive."

"Well, it's up to you," Pots said. "Take it or leave it."

Pots had the only insurance business for nearly thirty miles. Dad said he used that to keep the price up.

I stood in the open doorway and looked at the men. I was wondering what it felt like to be a chicken.

Mr. Norman rubbed his neck again.

Pots folded up his glasses, slid them into his shirt pocket, and turned to me. His eyes were small and black.

Mr. Norman looked, too. He blinked about six times, trying to clear the chaff from his eyes, I expect.

"Hello, lad," Mr. Norman said.

"Well, if it isn't Little Willy Yellowfly." Pots got up and stood with one hand on the open door. "Do you plan to buy some insurance?"

"No, I'm looking for Woody."

"Do you see him here?"

"No," I said.

"Well, bugger off then," he said, and slammed the door. A cloud of dust and chaff rushed past me and out into the street. Leaning against the sill was a nickel. As I bent down to pick it up, I could hear Pots's voice behind the door. "He's half Indian, I tell you. A damned half-Indian pissant."

"They're just boys playing," Mr. Norman said. "They'll get over it."

I walked and thought about Mr. Norman's words. I figured he meant me and Arthur would grow out of our friendship — like every other Indian kid and white kid had done for the past hundred years.

"I won't let it happen without a fight." I said it like Arthur was here with me, and I didn't care if Pots heard.

As I shuffled up the street, I wondered if Arthur was waiting for me in the bushes outside Heavy Shield School. Maybe he was thinking I had forgot about my promise to help him find *Kaxtomo*. Arthur was always telling me it was in the white man's nature to make a promise, then later find a way around it.

I went back to looking for Woody and for Dad's piece of metal. Mr. Wong was weeding his garden behind the Grayson café. He didn't seem to be mad at any kids, and his garden wasn't all ripped up. So I figured Woody was someplace else.

Next came Phillips's hardware. Mr. Phillips wasn't there, neither was Woody. But Sammy was. He was dancing with a corn broom. He made a big spin and held the broom way out with one hand, and together they bowed to the guns and fishing rods.

Oh boy, I thought. Now I've made trouble for Mary.

I decided to come back later and talk to Sammy about Mary. For now I continued up the street. At the hotel, I could smell cigarette smoke and beer. I opened the beer parlor door. Inside was a second door. Behind it, a man was singing about the war.

"Three German soldiers crossed the Rhine ..." He sang some more words. They were awfully dirty.

"Shut up, you old fool," another voice hollered.

I closed the door. Woody was too young to be in the beer parlor. But the laughing and hollering and cussing sounded like Woody's dad, Albert Loewan, who got beat up by Yellowfly in the big fight last spring. He was usually in the beer parlor when he wasn't working as foreman for Mr. Howe. He was one of the beer parlor men.

I turned my back to the door and looked across Main Street. The dirt path started at the beer parlor door and went past Mr. Gunther's new cars and trucks and over the tracks to Happy Valley, like somebody had drawn a line along a giant ruler. And even on the gravel of Main Street, with cars and trucks and some horses and wagons crossing over it all day long, the path was still there, joining the town to the reserve.

I looked past them all, down the giant ruler line, out onto the reserve, and up to where the road ended two miles from town. Heavy Shield School stood tall and rigid, made from hard, red bricks, named after a great Indian chief, and full of white men working day and night turning Indians away from what made them Indian.

Behind me, Singing Man started another chorus about the war.

I turned back to the beer parlor door.

Yellowfly had been a soldier in the war. In France, he had even been a hero. But in Grayson, people never noticed if an Indian was a hero. They only noticed if an Indian was a drunk.

Next came the beauty parlor. Woody wasn't there either. It was just for girls. But Mrs. Nolan was there. She was making Mrs. Phillips look pretty.

I gave a polite smile and a quick wave.

"Hi, Will," Mrs. Nolan said through the open door.

The bank was next. It was closed.

I looked at the sun. It was sitting at about five o'clock. If I found the piece of metal, maybe I could catch a ride home with Dad. He finished at six. I would have to hoe potatoes and study some for the tests on Wednesday.

I thought about Arthur again. He had to study, too. I wondered what kind of questions would be on a test an Indian would have to pass to be a white man. I wondered if Macleod had put something in the big No-Treaty that said "No pass: no white man."

Behind the bank was the Legion. Veterans came to drink beer after supper and talk about the war, and maybe sing dirty songs, too. All the veterans from all the wars could go to the Legion. Only Indians couldn't go, not even the ones who had fought in the war, not even heroes.

I turned right and went down the alley behind the beer parlor. The smell of beer came back, and so did my thoughts about tests. I figured if I was Arthur, I would try really hard to pass my tests. I could see no advantage to staying an Indian.

Singing Man was at it again, wearing out the German song.

Between the hotel and the alley was the big tin beer shed. Close to the shed were some stairs that went up the back of the hotel to a landing on the second floor. Off the landing were some rooms. A window was open in one. A ragged curtain hung, still, in the smelly air.

I leaned against the cool tin, wiped the sweat off my face, and listened to the grumbling men. Between the grumbles came, "Hey, how about a drink for an old soldier?"

I slipped into the shadows under the stairs and listened.

The singing stopped.

"You got something for me?" Singing Man said. "You don't get beer for nothing."

I crouched down close to the corner and peeked around a thick clump of foxtail growing up between the stairs. The back door was partly closed on a pair of feet. The rest of him was sitting on the floor just inside the beer parlor.

"I got something for you," the first voice said. He pushed open the door and picked up Dad's piece of red steel and held it up so Singing Man could see.

It was Woody.

I pulled back with a jerk.

"Ha," Singing Man said. "You'll need more than that to get a beer outta me."

Woody laughed, then he dug around in his pocket and gave Singing Man a nickel.

Singing Man handed Woody his beer and called, "Hey, bartender, where the hell's my beer?"

Woody slid out onto the ground, let the door close, and rested the piece of steel on his leg. After a minute, Woody opened the door, sat on the sill and leaned against the jamb.

"No heroes came outta the last war," Singing Man said. "All the real soldiers fought in the first war. All the real heroes came outta those trenches. Your pap was there, Pots was there, and I was there. We showed those Germans who could fight. And we can still fight. You wanna try me, I'm ready."

Woody drank a mouthful of beer and listened.

Singing Man bragged about the first war, how it was worse than any war would ever be, how every man in those damned trenches had been a hero.

Woody drank the rest of the beer, picked up the piece of steel, and held it like a bat. The beer and the steel were making Woody feel pretty tough, like maybe he thought he could beat an old soldier.

Singing Man took off his hat. His head came into the light of the open door. A long scar cut across his head above his ear. It looked like it hadn't grown hair in years.

"Got this in the trenches," he said.

Woody waved the steel.

"Go ahead, use it," Singing Man said. "I fought tougher men in those damn trenches." He took a long sloppy drink and choked. "Go ahead. Show me you're a hero."

He pulled on his hat and jerked his head back into the gray shadows coming from inside. He was getting madder and madder as he got drunker.

Woody put down his piece of steel and was pretty quiet.

Singing Man let out a big laugh like all the madness was just a joke. He swatted Woody with his hat and set a full glass of beer by Woody's elbow.

Woody laughed, too.

The piece of red steel leaned against the wall near the door, and for a while longer they were buddies again. They talked and drank beer. Singing Man complained about how miserable he felt, how it seemed that since the second war everybody had forgot about all the old soldiers, and how the old soldiers even forgot about one another.

He took a big drink and held up his beer. "But I've still got my best friend right here. The rest can go to hell."

From back in the beer parlor, the angry man shouted, "Hey, you, kid! Get outta here or I'll call the Mounties!"

Woody jumped up and quickly looked around. He turned back to the door, grabbed the glass of beer, and gulped down a big mouthful. He wiped his sleeve across his mouth and looked out into the alley.

I was flat on the ground under the stairs.

Now Woody had the piece of metal in one hand and the beer glass in the other. His face was red, and his eyes looked a little wild.

I swallowed hard.

He stepped away from the door and threw the beer glass. It made a tumbling stream of white foam and landed in some weeds behind the Legion.

I could see all of him now. He had long arms and wide, hard shoulders. He looked like his dad. He walked out another five paces and threw the piece of metal into the tall weeds not far from where the beer glass had landed.

I watched his boots through the space between the bottom step and the ground. They had extra long laces that were wrapped around his ankles about four eyelets down from the tops. He turned and headed up the alley to Frankie's store. I waited till I was sure he was gone, then I crawled out from under the stairs and the shadows and the foxtail grass.

I brushed off the dirt and hunted around in the weeds for Dad's swather part. I found the beer glass first. Then I saw the piece of steel sticking out of the tall grass growing along the sewer ditch. I had to pull pretty hard to get it out of the ground.

On the way back to Dad, I carried the piece of red steel like Woody had — holding it at one end like it was a club. That gave me an awful thought. Maybe it was Woody who beat up Yellowfly. Maybe he was *Kaxtomo*.

He Was Working Up His Nerve

Tuesday was a review day for reading and writing and spelling. Mr. Parks was writing on the blackboard, and I was daydreaming about fishing at Arrow Flats. I had just hooked a big pike and was about to pull it up the bank when Mr. Parks turned and stared right at me.

"Well?" he asked.

The skin on my neck got hot. My brain froze. I tried to buy some time with a thoughtful stare, like I was thinking. It didn't work.

He pointed to the question. "Well?" he asked again.

My eyes jerked back and forth over the words. They didn't make much sense reading them in two directions at once. As best I could figure, there was a fisherman or maybe it was a pike standing on a rock by the river and one of them was holding a new fishing rod. Then there was a question: "What is wrong with this sentence?"

"Mr. Samson, we are waiting," Mr. Parks said.

"He would have better luck catching a pike at Arrow Flats, not at the river," I said quickly.

A bunch of kids snickered.

Mr. Parks folded his hands behind his back. "Read the sentence aloud, please."

"The fisherman fought the thrashing pike standing on the river rock holding a new fishing rod," I read.

My face felt like it was on fire. I looked around the class. All the kids were considering the sentence. Even Woody was looking at it and scratching his head with his pencil.

"I see," Mr. Parks said, and looked away from me. "Would anyone else like to give it a try?"

A few hands went up. Mr. Parks picked Sammy. He had a good answer. Mr. Parks suggested another way to arrange the sentence. And in that one, Sammy pointed out a misspelled word and some poor grammar on Mr. Parks's part.

"Very good, Sammy," Mr. Parks said, then looked back at me. "It helps to pay attention."

Sammy agreed.

Mr. Parks went to the far corner of the blackboard and started writing. I read carefully just in case, but it wasn't much of a sentence. It read "There will be an essay on the test."

Freddie Cooper put his hand up and said, "Essay is spelled wrong."

Half the class snickered and half the class read the sentence again.

"No, it isn't, Freddie. But good try." Mr. Parks drew a line under the sentence. "This is a bonus question. You may write on whatever you like. You may even work on it at home. But you may not bring any written work into the test."

Half the class groaned and half the class was busy writing.

Mr. Parks talked about how to write a good paragraph, then about how to write a whole bunch of paragraphs that were called an essay or maybe a story.

Freddie Cooper stuck his hand up again. "Oh. Oh," he said.

I figured there was a problem with Mr. Parks's spelling or maybe Freddie had to go pee.

"Yes, Freddie?" Mr. Parks asked.

"Can I write about putting together International farm machinery?" he asked.

"Only if it's red."

Freddie got a funny look on his face, then he laughed. "International machinery has always been red," he said.

"Thank you, Freddie," Mr. Parks said. He looked around the class. "Does anyone else have a question?"

"Can I write about making antipasto?" Mary asked.

"That would be delicious."

Sammy didn't even put up his hand. He just burst out with, "I'll write a story about my girlfriend."

Everybody laughed, except Mary.

A bunch of hands shot up.

Mr. Parks waved his hands. "Write whatever you like," he said. "Make up a story or write a true story. Just write well."

I didn't put up my hand. I didn't have anything in my head worth putting on paper. I was a poor writer and a poor reader, and I was the worst speller in our class.

I was daydreaming again when Mr. Parks said, "Sammy."

Sammy was grinning and whispering to the kids around him. I hadn't seen Sammy so happy since grade five — when Woody was sitting someplace else.

"Gee, Mary," Sammy said. "You sure smell pretty today."

"Oh, thank you," Mary said.

Mary was nice to everybody.

During the rest of the morning, I watched Woody. At recess, I followed him around, always staying close enough to hear and see. I listened to every whisper. He didn't say a word about how he'd beat up Yellowfly. He was too busy tormenting Sammy.

At noon, we all went to the lunch room. Mary sat by the door. Sammy sat on the long bench under the windows. And I sat beside Sammy. I was afraid he would do something foolish, like go up to Mary and say, "Will said you like me. Want a nickel?" Then Mary would say back, "You're nice, Sammy, but I never said I like you, so I guess I can't take your nickel." After that, he'd never tell me who bought the fifty gopher tails.

Sammy took a bite of his sandwich, then turned to me and whispered something about Mary.

I just nodded because I couldn't hear him too good. I was chewing my lettuce sandwich.

Then Sammy opened his lunch box and took out an Orange Crush. He took another bite of his sandwich, he looked at Mary, then he looked at the Orange Crush.

Oh no, I thought. He's working up his nerve.

I had just taken a big bite of bread and lettuce when I heard Woody come marching down the stairs. Mary didn't hear Woody. She just looked over at me and Sammy and smiled. That's all Sammy needed. I looked away in time to see Woody kick the door open. A second later, Sammy was standing in front of Mary.

"Do you want my Orange Crush, Mary?" he asked. "I bought it just for you."

Mary crinkled up her nose like most kids do when Sammy gets too close, but instead of shooing him away, she said, "Oh yes, thank you."

Woody gave Sammy a mean stare and walked right up to him.

Mary was holding her hand out. She looked like a movie star. I thought Sammy was going to kiss her hand.

"Gimme me that soda," Woody said, and jerked Sammy around.

Sammy looked over his shoulder at Mary and then at Woody.

"I'll beat you up," Woody said.

Sammy started to shake.

"If you wreck the fizz in my soda," Woody said. "I'll —" Woody grabbed the Orange Crush with one hand and hit Sammy in the chest with the other.

Sammy fell backward and almost landed on Mary's foot. He rolled over and tried to stand.

Woody hooked Sammy's arm with the toe of his boot and pulled it out from under him.

Sammy landed flat on his face, with his legs pointing right at Mary.

Woody flicked the cap off with a quick snap of his belt buckle. Then he tipped the bottle to his lips and drained it.

Sammy looked at Mary. His face twisted into a silent, breathless cry.

Woody hooked his belt and smacked his lips. "Thanks for the soda, Sammy Boy." He dropped the bottle on the back of Sammy's legs and looked around to see if the other kids were watching.

Sammy turned to the floor and cried.

Sammy's Got Trouble

I was in the lumberyard hiding behind a stack of split cedar fence posts when Sammy ran past. He was looking back, but he was running full out. A few seconds later, Woody turned the corner, stopped, made a big Orange Crush burp, and followed Sammy.

I watched as they headed down Grierson Street to Frankie's store. Woody was sneaking along keeping the old poplars between himself and Sammy. He wasn't sneaking because he had to. He was doing it just to torment Sammy. Woody made a loud laugh every time he ducked behind a tree. After the second laugh, Sammy had stopped looking where he was going. But he still managed to turn the corner by Frankie's store.

Then his luck ended.

Jane Howe was driving her new Dodge car. She had just turned to park in front of Frankie's store when Sammy ran off the sidewalk. Sammy and the car got to the curb at the same time.

The car stopped.

Sammy didn't. He bounced and landed right back on the sidewalk.

"Oh, my God!" Jane Howe said.

Sammy jumped to his feet and tore off up the sidewalk.

"I'll give you a ride," she called after him.

Sammy didn't answer. He was escaping.

Woody ran to Frankie's corner and stopped. "Hi, Miss Howe," he said.

"Woody, I think I just hit Sammy Phillips."

"That's nice," he said.

I ran to the first poplar. The tree was big enough to hide me and then some. Frankie's roof sloped down toward the alley and blocked most of Cooper's yard. The back end of our old pickup stuck out into the alley. I didn't need to see Dad to know what he was doing. He would be standing in Cooper's machinery yard near the sidewalk, his hands on his hips, his hat sitting crooked on his head, and a cigarette hanging out of his mouth. He would be guarding his piles of steel.

I looked, then ran to the next tree.

I got to within one tree from Frankie's store and Woody. Woody was acting like he had nothing to do but hang around.

I ran to Frankie's store and took a quick look around the corner. Jane Howe was checking the grill on her new Dodge. There was no sign of Sammy.

Woody was shuffling past Mr. Cooper's yard. He had his hands in his pockets and he was whistling.

"If you touch so much as a washer, you little fart," Dad hollered, "I'll tan your thievin' hide!"

I pulled back. I figured Sammy had got to his dad's hardware safely. I allowed Dad a few seconds to stop cussing, then I quickly checked the sidewalk. Woody had wandered up the street and was hanging around Mr. Wong's café. He jerked around as if he knew I was watching him.

I pulled back again and pushed my shoulders flat against the wall.

Jane Howe stuck her head around the corner and stared at me. Her eyes were big and round, and she looked like she was winding herself up for a good cry.

"I think I hit Sammy Phillips with my car."

"Hi, Miss Howe."

"Didn't you hear me?"

"You didn't hurt Sammy. You helped him. If Woody had've got to him ahead of you, he'd'a beat him up. And Sammy would be sitting in the street crying by now."

"You wouldn't lie, just to make me feel better?"

"No, ma'am."

"You're the Samson boy?" she asked.

"Yes, ma'am."

She pulled her head back around the corner, and a few seconds later I heard her say, "Hi, Jim Samson."

Dad mumbled.

"That's a fine-looking swather you're building."
She made a little whistle. "Fine, indeed."

Dad mumbled again.

"Why no, Jim, I haven't seen your youngest boy,"
she said. "If I do, I'll be sure to let him know you
could use a hand. And don't worry about Woody. I'll
give you a shout if he comes back."

Dad made an extra long mumble and started
pounding on something that made a awfully loud
noise.

I didn't dare get closer to Mr. Cooper's yard in case
Dad came out to the sidewalk to holler at Woody
again. If Dad caught me, he'd put me to work. If
Woody caught me, he'd beat me up. I didn't know
which was worse. Anyway, I figured Woody was up
to something mean. I was afraid he'd steal a piece of
Mr. Cooper's swather and use it to beat up Sammy.

When Jane Howe stuck her head around the
corner again, I jumped. "Sorry. I just came to say
Woody's inside Pots's office," she said, then looked at
my face. "Are you Will or Tim?"

"Will," I said.

"You're the one who's friends with that Indian
boy?"

"Arthur," I said. "He's in school still; otherwise
he'd be here helping me —" I stopped before I said
too much.

Her eyes had pretty much lost their going-to-cry red color and her face had taken on an overall thoughtful look. "I don't like what they're doing to the Indian kids at Heavy Shield School. I believe in letting people choose their own path."

"I guess so, Miss Howe," I said, and glanced between her arm and the wall.

Mr. Phillips came out of the hardware and headed down the street to Mr. Wong's café. Now Sammy was alone.

"Maybe I could help you in Arthur's place," she said.

"Okay," I said.

She walked back to her car, bent over, and acted like she was checking her grill for Sammy dents. "Woody's outside now. He's standing in front of Pots's door. He's watching Mr. Phillips go into the café. Uh-oh, I believe Sammy has got himself the trouble you were talking about."

When I looked around the corner, Woody was disappearing into the hardware. I walked onto the sidewalk and headed toward Jane Howe.

She put her finger on her lips and pointed to the yard where Dad was working.

I nodded and whispered, "Nice Dodge, Miss Howe."

"Thank you, Will Samson," she whispered back.

Maybe I should've said I was Tim.

I pushed the door open and ducked inside. Mr. Cooper was working at the counter. He didn't look up.

I went down the hall, past the parts counter, and out into the workshop. The mechanic was there, grinding a piece of steel at the work bench. He didn't look up either.

I opened the small side door and peeked through the crack. Dad had stopped pounding and was looking toward the street just like I'd figured. I cleared my throat and, with my best Howard Cooper voice, called through the opening, "Jim Samson, get in here!" I coughed from the tickle that the coarse sound made in my throat.

Dad brushed the dirt off his hands and walked to the side door.

The mechanic was still grinding.

I ran back past the parts counter and grabbed a red International cap that was hanging on a hook. I pulled it down, almost over my eyes, and walked past Mr. Cooper out onto the sidewalk.

I stopped at the edge of the yard. The red parts were in their piles, but they were farther back than yesterday. Jane Howe stood in front of her black Dodge.

The little side door banged closed behind Dad.

I tossed the cap on the ground in front of Mr. Cooper's door. I figured the first place Dad would go was to Mr. Cooper, then out onto the sidewalk, where he would see the hat and stop to pick it up. That should slow him enough for me to get out of sight.

I was halfway through the yard when I heard Jane Howe say, "Hello, Jim Samson. Is that your hat?" She was nicer than her dad, Old Man Howe, and a lot sneakier.

I jumped the last pile of parts and ran down the alley to the hardware. The back door was made of metal, with rollers on the bottom and a big steel handle.

I leaned against the door, took a deep breath, and reached for the handle. It was hot from the afternoon sun. For a second, I thought how Woody had talked to Singing Man at the beer parlor and how he'd drunk beer like a man. It was then that I considered going home. I even hoped the door was locked, then I'd have an excuse for leaving Sammy to Woody.

I blew my air out and pulled on the handle. It clicked and moved with my hand. The door opened smooth and quiet.

I slipped in and crawled through the dark warehouse, around stovepipes, sheets of glass, drums of coal oil, and on to a dusty piece of light where the hardware started.

Woody was standing at the front counter where Mr. Phillips usually stands. I was too far away to hear exact words. But I knew what Woody was doing. I'd watched him do it all day. He was tormenting Sammy.

Now Woody's voice was loud.

Sammy never spoke. He just nodded and reached under the counter.

I stayed frozen in the piece of light.

"Give it to me!" Woody shouted.

Sammy pulled out an old shoe box.

I'd seen the box before. That's where Mr. Phillips kept the gopher tails and the money.

Woody hollered something dirty.

Sammy dropped the box, then turned and picked it up.

Woody slapped Sammy on the back of the head.

Sammy screamed.

Gopher tails flew everywhere — on the counter, on the floor, one even landed in Sammy's hair.

Woody grabbed handfuls of tails and stuffed his pockets. Then he knocked the box onto the floor and pushed Sammy down. Woody walked out the front door, nice and easy — like a big shot.

When I got to Sammy, he was sitting on the floor crying. He had landed on the shoe box and squashed it flat. He looked at me, his face all twisted up. Big tears rolled down his cheeks.

"Mary hates me," he said.

I sat on the floor beside him. I knew I should be following Woody. It was my chance to prove he beat up Yellowfly. But I couldn't leave Sammy.

Kids Were Turning
against Him

Sammy made a *hicka hicka* sound. That meant the worst of the crying was over. Good thing, because I was getting another backbone groove from leaning against the corner of Mr. Phillips's counter.

As I sat there, I thought about Woody. Not only was he a bully and a beer drinker and maybe even an Indian beater, now he was a robber, too. It was a good thing for Woody that Arthur hadn't seen Woody do all his mean things. Arthur wouldn't stand for it. He would fight Woody. I didn't know if Arthur would win or not, but I knew he would try. I wished Arthur was here, not at Heavy Shield School where everybody was a bully worse than Woody Loewan.

Sammy made another *hicka hicka* sound.

I put my hand on his knee like Mom did to me when she was trying to make me feel better about something I didn't think would ever go away. "We should get up before your dad comes back," I said.

"Yeah," he said between *hickas*.

That's when I saw the gopher tail peeking from Sammy's messed-up hair. I pulled it out and handed it to him. "Gotta cent?" I asked.

He sighed and grabbed the tail.

I wouldn't let go.

"Are you giving it to me, or not?"

"Not without a cent."

Sammy got a cross look, then gave the tail a big jerk.

I let go.

Sammy fell backward into a stack of corn brooms standing upside down in an old cream can.

The can wobbled.

Sammy grabbed it, missed with one hand, and hit it flat on the belly with the other.

The can leaned like a boxer trying to keep from falling, took a hard turn, and wobbled past me out into the center aisle. The brooms made a circular motion on their way by.

I waved back just to be sociable.

Sammy shot past me on his hands and knees. It looked like he was going to get the can in a headlock, but he just missed, and came up with an armload of brooms.

The can rolled between two big display tables.

"It's getting away," I called.

Sammy dropped the brooms and chased the can, knocking down stuff all over the store.

I picked up the squashed shoe box and stood behind the counter. "When you're done wrecking the place," I hollered over the noise. "I'll take a can of strychnine. I know a rat that needs poisoning."

"You'll need two cans!" he hollered back. "If it's the same rat I know."

There was a loud crash and a cuss and Sammy came out. He had a flat piece of stovepipe in one hand and was dragging the cream can with the other.

I dropped the box on the counter. "That was a job, but I got'er fixed."

Sammy cleaned up his mess, and I worked on Woody's. I still didn't know who got the fifty gopher tails and tied them in a circle, but I was getting mighty suspicious of Woody. Trying to get information out of Sammy right now seemed like a mean thing to do. I decided to work on fixing things for him and Mary.

Sammy was leaning on the stovepipe trying to make it round again when he said, "Promise me you won't say anything to anybody."

"About Woody?"

"Yeah."

"Okay. I promise."

I held one end of the pipe so it wouldn't roll, and Sammy gave it a good smack with his fist.

"Sammy," I said, "I can help you with Mary."

He reached into his pocket and took out his jackknife. He flipped open a dull blade and pried apart a seam on the pipe. He wouldn't look up.

I started acting confident again. "I can fix it for you and Mary," I said, snapping my fingers. "Just like that."

Sammy shook his head slowly as he worked his knife down the seam. "No," he said quietly. "I wrecked it. Mary hates me."

I didn't listen. "Here's how," I said, and plowed on. "Just wash good and put on some of your dad's aftershave. You'll smell nice. Girls like that."

Sammy let go of the pipe and glared at me. A second later he did something I'd never seen before. He got really mad. "I don't stink because I'm dirty!" he shouted right in my face.

"How come you stink then?"

He jammed his hand into his pocket, pulled out six gopher tails, and waved them in front of my nose. "That's how come," he hollered

"Well, don't put them in your pocket." I pushed his hand away. "Put them in the shoe box."

"I have to keep them in my pocket."

"Well, wrap them in some Eaton's paper, or anything to keep the smell down."

"You don't know —"

"Sure I know," I said. "I'll show you." I reached under Mr. Phillips's counter and pulled out a paper bag. Then I grabbed the tails.

Sammy gave the jackknife a quick flip, grabbed the dull blade, and snapped the handle across the back of my hand.

I jumped and dropped the tails.

Sammy bent over right in front of me and picked them up one by one and put them back into his pocket. That got me mad.

"You can't make Mary like you if you keep those stinky tails in your pocket!"

"I have to," he said. "Woody will beat me up if I don't."

"What? Woody wants you to stink?"

"So all the other kids will tease me at school."

"Well, don't take them to school, then."

"You're stupid, Will Samson. Didn't you hear me when I said I have to?"

I rubbed the lump the knife had made on my hand.

"I give them to Woody, one at a time, so he won't beat me up," Sammy said quietly to the floor.

"Oh, Sammy," I said.

"And the next day he comes back and gets his cent — or two or three." Sammy's voice got shaky. "And he always waits till Dad's there to see."

"Sammy, I didn't —"

"And Dad pats me on the back and says, 'Say thank you to your customer, son.'" The muscles in Sammy's jaw tightened. "Right in front of Woody and everybody."

I stood there not saying a word, thinking about the last year. Sammy spent the whole time trying to protect himself from a bully. And while he was doing it, the other kids were turning against him.

Darn You — Don't Run!

I stood behind the bank and rubbed the lump on my hand. The alley was hot and still. An Indian dog looked up from a knocked-over garbage can, gave me a little growl, then went back to his supper.

"Where are you, Woody?"

As I started down the middle of the alley, I glanced at the second-floor rooms, then ducked into the shadow of the beer shed. There I pressed my back against the cool metal and listened. It was quiet. From the corner of my eye I could see the ragged curtain hanging in the second-floor window. It was open and silent. The smell of beer drifted from the beer parlor.

Okay, let's have a look.

I sopped up the sweat from my forehead, hitched up my pants, then ran for the door.

The gravel crunched and popped under my feet.

The Indian dog jumped and shot down the alley.

I dropped to the ground and scrambled up to the door. It was open enough to slide a beer bottle through. From inside came the low grumble of drinking men and the rattle of glasses. The room was dark and smoky. There was no Woody. But Singing Man sat close to the door. He wore big old army boots — the ones that lace up high. His shirt sleeve hung flat and still by his side like the curtain in the second-floor room. At the bottom of the sleeve where his hand should have been, there was nothing at all.

I'd known for about a year now that one of the beer parlor men had only one arm, but it still gave me the willies to see it, and it kind of made my right arm hurt.

I slowly slid the door open and stuck my head inside.

Singing Man's face was turned to the smoke. He mumbled some dirty words about the wine and the women and the war. Then he started to sing.

"Shut up, you old fool!" a man hollered through the smoke.

"You son of a —" Singing Man cussed. "I'll sing if I wanna."

"You'll shut up if I tell you!" the man called back.

"I was in those damned trenches," Singing Man said. "I earned the right to sing whatever I wanna, whenever I wanna."

"What trench would that be?" the man called out, then laughed. "The one in Happy Valley?"

A bunch of beer parlor men let out a big laugh.

Singing Man took a drag on his cigarette, blew out the smoke, grabbed his glass of beer, and took a big sloppy drink.

The cigarette sizzled on his face.

He jerked his hand away. A splash of beer hit the table and ran onto the floor. He tossed his cigarette into the puddle of beer, stomped it, then cussed the people who first made them.

Now the room smelled like burning hair and skin mixed with cigarette smoke and beer.

A second later, Singing Man was looking right at me.

I could see his face clearly. He had a pretty good burn from the cigarette. He had plenty more just like it. There were lots of little bald spots where the gray and black stubble had gotten burned out.

"What're you lookin' at, Indian?" His eyes were mostly closed. "You think yer tough. I'll show you who's tough. Damn you and Happy Valley. I fought in those trenches." He kicked at me with one of his big boots.

I tried to pull away, but I was too slow. His kick caught the door, slammed it into my sore nose, and knocked me backward into the dirt.

I rolled onto my side and shook my head.

The door swung fully open, hit the wall, and jumped back. Singing Man stood, squinting into the light. He jerked the door closed and cussed through it — one cuss for me and one cuss for the cigarette.

I sat in the dirt for a while and gently held my nose so it wouldn't bleed all over my shirt. I wiggled it carefully and felt a little click.

When I could see straight, I took a deep breath and got up. My head spun. I leaned over, took another breath, and swallowed. My mouth tasted like dirty beer. My stomach rolled.

I reached out one hand and wobbled to the beer shed. There, I leaned against the cool metal and sunk to the ground. Behind the beer parlor door, the singing started again. I hated that stupid song.

I held my hands over my ears. My nose dripped. I pinched it.

"Three German soldiers —"

"Ah, shut up."

"Jeez," I said, pulling myself up and staggering down the alley.

The dog peeked out from where he was hiding and gave me a low growl.

"Oh, go eat your supper," I said.

I wobbled on, holding my nose and swallowing. At Mr. Cooper's yard, Dad was bent over the swather. His head was pointing toward Main Street. His other end was pointing toward me. On guard, I guess.

I slipped past the yard and around to the front of Frankie's store. The jawbreaker machine sat all alone in the corner.

Woody wasn't around.

I figured now was a good time to tell Sergeant Findley about Woody, at least about how he'd robbed Sammy's gopher tail business. I didn't know if Woody had beat up Yellowfly, but I knew what he'd done to Sammy. There was only one thing getting in the way. I had promised Sammy I wouldn't tell.

I was looking in Frankie's window when I saw the reflection of the Mountie's car.

Sergeant Findley pulled up behind me and parked. "Darn you — don't run from me again!" he shouted. A second later, his car door opened and closed.

When I turned, Sergeant Findley was sitting on his fender with one foot resting on the bumper and the other on the ground.

"You run again, and I'll throw you in jail," he said, looking at my nose. "What the hell happened to you?"

This was my chance to get out of this mess forever. No one would blame me for telling the truth to a Mountie. But I just stared at him.

He lifted his hat and wiped up some sweat. Then he shifted his belt. His gun moved to the front.

I wondered what he would do if I was an Indian. I bet I would be in jail by now. Then I wondered what Crowfoot would do if he was me. I thought about the No-Treaty and all the no-things Macleod put in it.

Sergeant Findley's mustache wiggled. "Answer me," he said.

"Nothing."

He got up, shifted his hat, and gave me a hard look. "Okay," he said. "If that's the way you want it, that's the way you'll get it."

If he was going to say anything else, I didn't wait around to hear. I just walked past him. He was still standing in the street when I got to the train station. I headed along the tracks to the Wheat Pool elevator, stopped, and looked back at the town. The Indian dog watched me from the alley behind the butcher shop.

I headed into Happy Valley.

A Circle of Gopher Tails

I left a trail of blood through the heavy dust and on in behind the Saskatoon bushes. I sat and held my nose. It felt like a ripe tomato.

Sergeant Findley drove past the beer parlor, turned north, and headed out of town.

I checked my nose again. It felt better if I left it alone.

I was eating Saskatoon berries and watching the streets for any sign of Woody when Dad came out of the beer parlor. He had a case of beer under each arm. Mr. Cooper and his men would be busy for a few hours. I could go see Arthur in peace.

I gave downtown one last check. A grain truck pulled out of the elevator. Mr. Norman stood at the top of the ramp and leaned on a coarse push broom.

I stood to wave to Mr. Norman and saw Woody sitting in one of Mr. Gunther's new Fargo trucks.

He looked right at me.

I dropped to the ground, wriggled up to the bushes, and peeked out.

Woody lowered his head and bent over, like he was reaching under the seat for the tire iron. Then the door opened and Woody stepped out and looked around. He was holding something, but I couldn't tell what.

There was no time to run. I'd have to hide. I pushed myself backward with my hands and elbows, passed through the grass to a small patch of heavy dust, held still for a second and listened.

It was quiet.

I got to my hands and knees and turned.

Woody was standing on the tracks, looking into Happy Valley.

I spun around and clawed at the ground.

Woody crunched through the rocks that held the rails.

Then it was quiet again.

His boots made little explosions in the heavy dust now. For a second, I could smell gopher tails.

Straight ahead was another clump of bushes. I shot through the weeds, jumped, and rolled behind the bushes. I looked back, taking long, quiet breaths. In the patch of dirt was the shape of my body and in that shape was a trail of Saskatoon berries.

Woody walked around the first bush, then he stopped and looked down at my shape in the dust.

I held my breath.

He bent over and, one by one, picked up the berries and ate them.

My heart pounded.

He turned his head and listened. He looked at the path, then at the tracks.

My head went all cloudy from lack of air, and in my mind I heard that stupid, stupid war song. But it wasn't singing I heard, it was whistling.

Woody turned back to the path.

I took a quick breath.

Woody was whistling. *Three German soldiers crossed the Rhine* ... On a finger, he was spinning something around and around.

It was a circle of gopher tails.

Watcher and His Brother

I crawled to the edge of my hiding place and watched Woody turn down the path, cross the narrow strip of CPR land, and walk out onto the reserve. He had robbed Sammy of his gopher tails and then broke into Mr. Gunther's Fargo truck — and that's where he made the tails into a circle. They were my proof. Now I knew Woody was involved with Yellowfly's beating, but I still didn't know why he wanted the gopher tails or what he was going to do with them. Then Arthur's voice came into my head as if he was lying in the bushes beside me: The circle was made for a special purpose.

I would have to follow Woody to find out what that was.

Woody walked straight up the road toward Heavy Shield School.

I let him get half a mile ahead, then I followed. I walked past the Indian Agent's office, the Indian Agent's house and the Indian hospital. They all looked pretty nice, with their mowed lawns and flowers in the windows and tall trees in the lanes. I didn't bother looking at the Indians' houses — they were just shacks.

Heavy Shield School was two miles from town. It was easy to find. All you had to do was walk out the front door of the beer parlor, go up the path through Happy Valley, and then straight up the road that goes no place else. That's Heavy Shield School, sitting on a hill overlooking the reserve.

Woody turned and looked toward me.

I stopped and made like I was an Indian kid — I kicked a rock, looked in the ditch, and slouched around.

Woody bent over, picked up a rock, and threw it.

A dog yelped and ran out of the ditch to one of the shacks. A second later, Woody was throwing handfuls of rocks and barking.

Now three dogs were yelping.

I was getting ready to cheer for the dogs when I heard a loud snort.

I turned and looked down the road. The dray pulled by those two miserable-looking horses plodded out from behind a clump of poplar suckers. It crossed the ditch, climbed up onto the road, pulled ahead of me and stopped. It was Watcher and His Brother. The same two Indian men who had given Arthur's mom and dad a ride home after church.

I looked up the road. Woody was running from about twenty Indian dogs.

Watcher reached back and slapped the planks.

I jumped on.

He gave the reins a snap and the horses let out a snort. The leather rubbed, and the wagon rattled and clanked. In a second the horses were huffing and puffing along, and the wheels were crunching and popping in the rocks.

I let my legs dangle over the edge.

Watcher and His Brother talked their Indian language.

I couldn't understand them, of course.

After a hundred yards, Watcher raised one leg and put it on the hitch. He was big. They were both big. Arthur's dad was big, so was his mom, so was his grandpa, and Arthur was bigger than me even though we were both twelve. Yellowfly was big, too. That's the way most Indians were.

Dad always said, "They're tough, too. It took two Germans to make a fair fight with one Indian. And usually the Indian won."

I considered that for a minute. Maybe Woody had been hiding behind the clump of Saskatoon bushes and surprised Yellowfly. Or maybe he'd had help. Two attackers made more sense when it came to fighting someone like Yellowfly.

I just had to think about him, and I was back in Happy Valley, hiding behind the Saskatoon bushes. Woody sat on one side and a big German soldier sat on the other. They were talking around me like I wasn't there. Woody threw his handful of rocks. The

German soldier jumped out from behind the Saskatoon bushes and hit Yellowfly with a piece of red steel from Mr. Cooper's swather.

I tried to holler, but all that came out was that German soldier song.

Watcher turned and stared at me. He had deep black eyes and a hard dark face.

I looked at the ditch.

He turned and snapped the reins.

The horses snorted.

There was nothing to look at now, just some shacks with lots of kids and dogs. The kids were wild, like olden days Indians, I expect. They were all little ones, too young for being changed into white men at Heavy Shield School. A half-grown dog peeked out from behind a woodpile and barked at me. I guess he was still mad at Woody, and was taking it out on me.

Now Watcher had both feet on the hitch. His arms rested easy on his legs, with the reins loose in his hands.

As His Brother talked, he made a sign by putting two fingers together on one hand and making a jerking motion down the road. He made the same sign with his other hand. Then he did both together — one behind the other.

It looked like two horses chasing each other.

Then he made a wiping sign, as if he'd just finished some pretty important business in the outhouse. After the wiping sign, he quickly flicked his hand, as if he was getting rid of something awfully dirty.

It looked like he'd gone to the outhouse but had forgotten to bring an Eaton's catalog for wiping, and so had to wipe with his bare hand.

Mixed in with his Indian words was Sergeant Findley's name.

I knew the wiping sign pretty good. I'd got it myself from Indian men who were mad at me for some reason. I figured it was a way to cuss a person who was too far away to hear a regular cuss.

Watcher nodded.

They both went back to staring down the road.

We were getting close to Heavy Shield School when Sergeant Findley went ripping past. Rocks flew everywhere. Some landed on the wagon. I could hardly see the horses for all the dust, but they didn't seem to be scared. They just clopped and puffed along.

His Brother made the chasing sign followed by the dirty sign again.

Watcher nodded.

I wondered if they were planning to chase Sergeant Findley with their horses, then when they saw how fast he was going, they decided to cuss him instead.

We turned on the dirt trail that ran west beside Heavy Shield School. I couldn't see Woody anywhere. I figured the dogs had chased him inside the school.

I gave the wagon two slaps and jumped off.

Watcher raised his hand but didn't look back. I could see "SIKSIKA," that name the Blackfoot call themselves, clearly written in bold letters on the shoulder of his army shirt.

His Brother made another dirty sign.

A cloud of dust followed Sergeant Findley.

Go Home, White Man

I stood in front of Heavy Shield School and looked up. It was tall and wide and long. The roof was flat with a ledge of gray concrete. The walls were red brick. The windows were small and dark. Extra wide stairs went to the second floor and stopped at a pair of big wooden doors. They were open. Inside was a second pair of doors. They were open, too. A tall, dark man passed the doors then disappeared.

In the chapel, kids were singing to Jesus.

High up on the ledge, a stone cross sat looking east across the reserve. Under the cross it said "1929."

The old Heavy Shield School burned down in 1928. It was made of wood. The new one was made of brick and stone. It would last forever.

Somewhere deep inside Heavy Shield School, the Anglicans were trying to turn Arthur into a white man.

"Hey, you!" a voice hollered. "What do you think you're doing?"

"I didn't do nothing," I said, looking around.

A supervisor walked over to where some Indian kids were pulling weeds from the flowers that grew along the front. He dragged a kid out from the flower bed and slapped his ear. "I told you a dozen times to be careful."

The kid rubbed his ear with one hand; in the other hand he had a long flower with the roots and some dirt still hanging in a ball. The kids were all too young for Arthur to be working with.

While the supervisor was hollering and slapping the first kid, two others got together and yanked out a really big flower.

"Damn your red hides!" the supervisor shouted. He left the first kid and took the two flower pullers by the ears, turned them, and marched them up the big stairs. "It's the strap for you two," he said.

While he was gone, the first kid got the others all worked up. They were laughing and calling each other "dumb Indian kids who would never amount to a hill of beans." When they got done acting like they were supervisors, they went back to weeding. It didn't take long before another flower got pulled out.

Around the back of the school was a big red barn.

Some kids were weeding vegetables and others were hoeing potatoes. The kids looked old enough for Arthur to be working with them. But he wasn't there. There was a kid who would rather pull out carrots than weeds. I figured he must have graduated from being a flower puller. He got sent for a strapping, too.

I was standing by the barn when the kid walked by. "Psst," I said, motioning for him to come over.

He checked to see if the supervisor was watching, then came over. "Yeah?"

"Where's Arthur?"

"Inside." He pointed at the barn. "He pulled out a potato."

"A whole potato?"

"Yeah," he said, grinning. "There were even little ones on the bottom."

Oh, brother, I thought. It's an uprising. I waved to the boy. "Thanks," I said, and headed for the big front doors.

"Not there, that's where the barn supervisor is. Go around the side door."

Then the potato supervisor hollered, "Hey, I thought I told you to go see Mr. Kratz." I guess Mr. Kratz was the strap supervisor.

The kid gave my nose a long look. "What happened to you? Did you run into a supervisor?"

"No, I bumped into a door."

"You must'a been going pretty fast."

"The door was moving, too."

He was nodding like he'd seen it before.

"What did I tell you?" the supervisor hollered.

"Gotta get my strap," the kid said to me, and rubbed his hands together.

I nodded like I'd seen it before.

I snuck around the barn to the side door and ducked inside. Arthur was bent over, looking through a knothole in the wall that divided the barn in half. Leaning against the wall was a scoop shovel. Beside him was an old wooden wagon. The wagon was overflowing with the sloppiest manure I ever saw. And it stunk, too, worse than a pocket full of gopher tails on the hottest day of the year.

I walked through the manure like I did it every day, got halfway, and gave Arthur a big friendly wave. "Hi, Arthur," I said. "What are you looking at?"

He waved at me to shut up, then motioned me over. "Don't make a sound," he whispered, and put a finger to his lips. He looked at my nose. "What's the other guy look like?"

"Worse," I whispered.

"Dead, I hope."

"Stone cold," I said.

He pointed to a knothole near his own. I looked through.

Woody was standing beside the barn supervisor. They were leaning on a steel railing with their elbows sitting easy on the top rung. When the supervisor moved one foot to the bottom rung, Woody did the same. Pretty soon they both had their hands crossed and their chins resting on them.

The supervisor wore brown cowboy boots and a brown cowboy hat pushed back on his head. If he was lucky, he was twenty years old. They looked like a couple of big shots.

Near the front doors, an Indian boy was shoveling manure into a tall wagon like the one Arthur was working with. He was about the same age as Arthur. I figured he was a carrot puller or maybe even a potato puller, and shoveling manure was his punishment.

"Okay," the supervisor said. "That's good." The boy had a hold on the wagon and was about to take it out to the manure pile and dump it when the supervisor said, "Hold on a minute. I've got something special for you." He gave Woody a pat on the shoulder and walked over to the boy.

Woody laughed.

The supervisor dug in his pocket as he walked.

Then he began whistling. *Three German soldiers crossed the Rhine ...* On one finger, he was spinning something around and around. It was the circle of gopher tails.

Woody was just about wetting his pants, he was laughing so hard.

My mouth fell open and I pulled back from the hole.

Arthur jerked away from his hole and looked at me. "Where'd he get those gopher tails?" He looked at me like he thought I gave our only clue to the supervisor.

"He got them from Woody," I said. "I still got the ones I showed you. Woody stole those from Sammy Phillips. I saw him do it. I was following him." I took a quick breath. "That's why I'm here. That's why I got this sore nose."

"So it was them who beat up Yellowfly," Arthur said.

Woody laughed again.

I glared through the knothole. "Look," I said.

The Indian boy was standing by his wagon of manure.

"This is for you," the supervisor said, holding out the circle of gopher tails. "Go ahead, take them."

The boy reached out his hand.

"Now put them on."

Woody was laughing louder than ever.

The boy untied the string that held the tails in a circle. Then he put them around his head and tied them. The tails stood straight up in a circle around the boy's head.

"*Kaxtomo*," Arthur whispered.

"There, now aren't you a real brave warrior," the supervisor said, glancing at Woody.

"It's a chief," Woody called between his laughs. "It's Chief Heavy Shield."

"Now take your wagon outside," the supervisor said. "And make sure all your friends see that you're such a nice-looking warrior."

"Chief! Chief!"

I felt sick and ashamed. But the boy wasn't. I would be crying by now. But he wasn't doing that, either. He was doing what he was told. He was hauling the wagon full of manure outside, wearing his stupid headdress. And all of his friends would see and maybe laugh at him. He pulled his wagon slowly to the manure pile. The supervisor didn't know it, but what he said was true — the boy was brave. Maybe as brave as Yellowfly.

"Why'd they do that?" I asked, half whispering and half crying.

"Shut up," Arthur said.

I didn't know what to say to that.

The supervisor walked back to Woody. He had a wide grin on his face, and when he got close to Woody, he winked at him.

"I hate them," Arthur said.

"Me, too," I said.

The supervisor and Woody stood like before, with their feet on the bottom rail.

The Indian boy worked hard to get the wagon outside without spilling anything.

The supervisor slapped Woody on the back like he was proud of what Woody had done. I hadn't seen Woody do anything except watch the meanness. Then Woody made a punch at the supervisor's side. But he stopped short. They were just fooling around, playing their mean game.

I heard a scraping sound behind me.

Arthur was busy shoveling more manure into the wagon. Then he grabbed a pail from behind the stall and poured some water into the wagon. Water and manure ran out the cracks and over the top. It was an awfully sloppy mess.

"You should slop the water on the floor," I said, and looked at the pail.

"Just shut up." Arthur said it loud, like he was talking to the supervisor or to Woody, like he didn't care who heard.

He threw the shovel down. It rattled and clanked into the corner. He kicked the pail into the corner, too. Then he pulled on the wagon. It was stuck. He pulled again. His feet flew up and he landed in the manure with his legs under the wagon. He got up, jerked on the handle, and fell again.

I tried to push the wagon to help get it moving, but he just yelled, "Leave me alone!"

He looked away, grabbed a post that held up the barn, and gave the wagon another hard jerk.

It started to move.

I followed behind him, ready to give it a push. But he didn't need me. I held up short of the opening in the wall that divided the barn. Arthur stopped with the wagon and blocked the corner stall where Woody and the supervisor stood.

"Get that out to the manure pile," the supervisor shouted.

"Yeah," Woody said.

Arthur had let the handle drop to the floor and was standing with the wagon between himself and the two big shots. "I said, get that to the —"

That's all the supervisor got out before Arthur planted his feet solid on the floor, grabbed hold of the wagon low on its side, gave it a heave, and let out a scream like I'd never heard before.

The wagon got to halfway, stood still for a second, then fell over on its side.

Woody's eyes were big and round, and his mouth was open.

I figured that was a mistake, considering how big the wagon was and how messy the manure was.

The supervisor scrunched up his face.

Then they jumped for the rail.

But it was too late. Arthur had them cornered.

The manure hit Woody and pushed him down and rolled right over him. It came back off the wall, pushed the supervisor down from behind, and slopped him right into the wagon.

The Indian boy let out a whoop and tossed the gopher tails to Arthur.

Arthur caught them and threw them at the supervisor. They landed half on his face and half on his hair. He looked like some kind of half-man half-manure fool.

The Indian boy let out another whoop and tipped over his wagon. It was a horrible mess.

Arthur and the boy ran past me like I wasn't even there.

"Come back here, you redskins!" the supervisor screamed.

Woody didn't say nothing. He just stood there, spitting.

I followed Arthur.

The potato supervisor ran by us into the barn.

Outside, the Indian boys formed a circle around Arthur and cheered for him like he was a hero. I couldn't understand the words because they yelled in Indian, but it didn't matter that much — I still felt proud of Arthur. He'd done just like Dad said Indians can do. He'd beat two to his one.

I tried to push into the circle and give Arthur a pat on the back, but the other boys wouldn't let me.

"Arthur," I called.

But he was in the middle of the noise.

I called for him again.

He still didn't hear me.

I pushed at the boys.

One boy broke from the crowd, grabbed me by my shirt, and shook me. "Go home, white man," he said, and pushed me.

I fell backward and landed in the dirt.

The crowd of Indian boys ran around the barn, still hollering and cheering.

"Arthur!" I called again.

No-Man's-Land

I sat on the rail with Grayson at my back and stared into Happy Valley. Two gophers scratched around looking for roots and seeds. I didn't see Woody or a German soldier or Arthur or even Yellowfly.

I picked up a rock and tossed it. It made a puff in the heavy dust and formed a circle like it was an explosion. The gophers jumped, then came back to the circle and looked over its edge.

I rolled another rock in my hand.

Arthur was mad at me for what Woody had done and what the supervisor had done. Maybe he didn't believe me. Maybe he thought it was me who gave the tails to Woody. If Arthur thought that then he would be more than mad at me, he would hate me.

I thought again about what Mr. Norman had said, how me and Arthur would outgrow being friends. Maybe that's what was happening. Maybe it was already too late.

Behind me, I heard Mr. Norman call to Mr. Gunther. "Good night, Gun."

"Good night, Walt," Mr. Gunther called back.

They sounded like friends.

I wished I'd been the one who had tipped over the manure wagon on Woody and the supervisor. Then maybe Arthur would think I was a good enough friend. Maybe the other Indian boys wouldn't have pushed me away and told me to go home.

I rolled the rock in my hand.

The gophers had gone back to looking for food. They were rooting around in the grass and ignoring me. I went to throw the rock, but I held up. I could've done it easy. I was a good shot with a rock. Yesterday I could've done it. But not anymore. I didn't even feel much like snaring gophers anymore. Snaring seemed like a mean thing to do. I couldn't even remember why everybody in Grayson thought gophers were so bad.

I looked along the narrow strip of CPR land, down the tracks toward Arthur's house, then up the tracks toward my house. There was no sign of trains and no sign of people of any kind. Dad called it no-man's-land because it wasn't part of the reserve or the town. It felt like the right place for a person who wasn't Indian enough for the reserve and wasn't white enough for the town. It felt like the right place for me.

I got up and turned to the town.

Mr. Norman's pickup was parked at the bottom of the ramp. The driver's door was open. It jiggled in time with the rough-running motor. Mr. Norman was standing in front of the grill. His pant leg fluttered like the fan was trying to suck him into the radiator. In his hand was one of Mr. Gunther's eye-popping green bottles of Coke.

He watched me cross the three sets of tracks. When I got in line with him, I stopped and looked at my feet.

"Did you mean what you said about me and Arthur outgrowing being friends?"

"No."

"How come you said it then?"

"It wasn't directed at you. I didn't mean for you to feel bad about it." Mr. Norman took a big breath. "You know Pots is a hard man. I was just trying to distract him from tormenting you. But it was a lie. I am sorry, Will."

I shrugged my shoulders like it wasn't a big deal. "Did you ever have an Indian friend?"

He held out the Coke. The bottle was open and all wet on the outside. "A few," he said. I took a big drink and rubbed my eyes. When I handed him back the bottle, he just shook his head. "I've had plenty already, but thanks for offering."

"Are you still friends now?" I asked, and took another swig.

"No," he said.

"Did they outgrow liking you?"

The pickup let out a cough, sputtered, then caught a spark and rumbled on.

"They died in the war."

"The first war?"

Mr. Norman nodded and held out his hand. "I could use a drink about now."

I gave him the bottle.

He drank a big gulp. His eyes went all cloudy and still. "Our artillery shelled the German trenches for three days. Then we charged out of our trenches. We thought we had 'em licked, but when we got halfway, their machine guns — well, you don't need to hear the rest." He took another drink and rubbed his sleeve across his lips. "No-man's-land, that's what that shelled-out strip between enemy lines was called. That's where my friends died. Don't ever get stuck in no-man's-land."

I looked at the bottle. It was empty.

"Sorry," he said.

He offered me a nickel, but I said I'd had plenty today. He put his hand on my shoulder and said no matter what the town or the reserve might think, friendship is worth more to the heart than mistrust or suspicion or hatred is to whatever part of the body needs those bad things.

Mr. Norman still had the Coke bottle by the neck when he climbed into his pickup and drove away.

I Made a Conclusion

I headed past Mr. Gunther's new cars and trucks. The beer parlor was emptying out. It was six o'clock and everybody in Grayson had to go home for supper, even the drunks. It'd open again at eight. Some of the beer parlor men would be hanging around by seven-thirty, crying about how the door should be open by now and, boy, they should fix their clock.

I walked along Main Street, around the corner by the bank, and down the alley. I thought about the first circle of gopher tails. I figured Woody must have robbed Sammy sometime before Saturday afternoon, when I found the tails in the Saskatoon bushes. I also figured he must have been on his way to Heavy Shield School to give the tails to the supervisor, so they could play their mean game on the Indian boy.

But Woody didn't get past the Saskatoon bushes before he dropped the circle of tails.

Then I thought about what could've happened to Yellowfly: Woody was hiding behind the Saskatoon bushes, tying his first bunch of stolen tails into a circle. Yellowfly came along the path from town. Somebody followed him into Happy Valley, beat him, and left him in the dirt. Woody saw it all, dropped the tails, and ran.

Nice and easy. But it didn't feel right. It would be pretty hard to sneak up on me in Happy Valley, so sneaking up on Yellowfly would be impossible. He must have been ambushed.

I stopped behind the bank.

Yellowfly was a hero — the toughest man on the reserve or in Grayson. I couldn't see one man ambushing him, and I was having a hard time with two men doing it, but if they did, I'd bet Woody was one of them.

I went over the whole thing one more time. This time I used the scientific method.

I made a hypothesis: Woody was there, but he wasn't alone.

I made an experiment: There were two of them watching Yellowfly as he walked down the path. Woody fell on the ground and moaned, "Oh, I got hit by a train. Oh, I'm hurt." Yellowfly went over, stopped, and bent down to help Woody. Woody looked up and grinned. Yellowfly knew he was ambushed, but it was too late. He was hit. He fell in the dirt. The two cowards ran. Me and Arthur came along the tracks.

I tried a conclusion: I was awfully suspicious of the supervisor, but I wasn't sure. He seemed like a coward, someone who'd just shame a kid. But there was one thing I *was* sure of: Woody knew who that second person was.

I guess it wasn't a simple conclusion, like Mr. Parks said they should be. I wondered if Galileo had problems with his conclusions, too.

I walked down the alley behind the hotel.

Singing Man came out with a case of beer tucked under his good arm. He crawled up the stairs and disappeared into the second-floor room.

The empty sleeve crossed in front of the window and stopped. Then the face looked out at me. It had a large, hard nose with sagging cheeks and puffy eyes. He looked worse in the daylight.

"What'er you lookin' at?" he grunted.

"I didn't do anything," I said.

"You want one of these?" He made a fist with his good hand and stuck it out the window. The fingers were yellow from cigarette smoke.

I figured he recognized my swollen nose from where he tried to kick it off, and he was getting ready to finish me with a punch. I ran down the alley till he was out of sight.

"I'll show you!" he cussed. "You half-Indian son of a —"

I tried not to listen.

At Mr. Cooper's shop, I could hear Dad and Mr. Cooper and the mechanic. They were arguing about how best to put together a swather. They sounded pretty drunk.

I walked into the yard and stood for a while looking at Dad's piles of metal. Woody and the supervisor and Singing Man were in my head. Over and over they sang. *Three German soldiers ...*

I picked up a piece of steel and held it like a bat, like Woody had done.

The words rolled over and over in my head.

Main Street was empty except for the black Dodge car parked in front of the library. Jane Howe stood behind the picture window. She was watching me, not like a person who's sneaking a look, but more like someone who doesn't care if they're seen.

I walked past Pots's insurance and headed slowly to the hardware.

Jane Howe moved from the picture window and looked out the window in the door. She had a book in her hand, and she was tapping it against her leg.

I stopped in front of the hardware and looked past the library to the spot on the railway tracks where the one track turned into three. When I looked back at the library, Jane Howe was gone from the window.

From up the alley, the sound of Singing Man's German song drifted out into the street. *Three German soldiers crossed the Rhine ...* I thought of Dad's words again: It took two Germans to make a fair fight with one Indian. And usually the Indian won.

I turned and walked back to Mr. Cooper's yard.

Now the song played over and over with Dad's words.

I stood in front of the half-put-together swather and looked down at the piece of steel in my hand. The red paint looked like blood. If Dad was right about Indians, then it would take more than two men to beat one Indian.

I got an awful shiver. "Oh boy," I said. "The German soldiers were *Kaxtomo*." Goose bumps lumped down my back. Hair stood up all over my body. "Oh darn, there were three of them. That's how they beat up Yellowfly."

Our Boys Return from the Trenches

The library usually closed at six o'clock like every-thing else in Grayson. But a sign hung from a nail above the window: Open.

I pushed the door and stepped in.

Jane Howe put her finger to her lips and made a shush sign.

I looked around as I walked past the tall book-shelves. There wasn't anybody else there. I stopped in front of her desk and stuck my hands in my pockets.

"Yes?" she said.

"What's the Rhine?"

"I only know of one. It's a river in Germany."

I asked about the song. She didn't know much about songs with so few words. I told her I could sing more, but they were pretty dirty. She said she would listen, but she stopped me before I finished. I was glad.

It was a war song, she said. Her dad would sing it when he'd had one too many.

I asked if it was from the first war.

She said most likely, but she wasn't a song expert.

I said thanks and headed for the shelves.

I walked up and down the rows of books till I found what I was looking for. I got an armload and sat down.

Jane Howe gave the shush sign again, then she smiled.

In a few minutes I had all the books open. The table was covered, and I was more confused than ever.

Jane Howe sat in the chair beside me and whispered, "Are you interested in the Great War?"

"No," I whispered back. "I'm interested in the first war."

She smiled and patted a picture of trenches and shell holes and dead horses. "The first war is the Great War."

I just nodded.

"Are you researching an exam question for Mr. Parks? I like to keep the library open on just such occasions."

I shook my head. "No, ma'am, I'm working on a conclusion. It's kind of scientific."

"Scientific," she said, and rested her hand on the picture of the shell hole. "What is your hypothesis, exactly?"

I couldn't say to her *Woody wasn't alone in Happy Valley*, so I said, "Ah, names."

"When I was in school a hypothesis was usually worded in the form of a statement. Of course, that was a long time ago, and things change."

"Names of the men who went to the first war."

She patted the dead horses and shook her head. "That's a lot of names."

"The men who went from Grayson."

"Well, that's a little better." She went to a shelf, rummaged around, and came back carrying one little book. She closed the page on the horse and she sat down. "I think this is the book you want."

On the cover it said, "The History of Grayson: 1900 to 1945." It looked like the same one she'd been tapping her leg with.

"If you have any more questions," she said, getting up, "I'll be reshelving all these." She gathered my pile of books into her arms and headed back to the war shelves.

I started reading. When I got to the pages on the first war, Jane Howe walked over to my table and put a piece of paper and a pencil in front of me. I read a long list of names of men from Grayson who died in the Great War. I had heard all the names before. I looked at pages of pictures, too — some of happy, young men wearing new uniforms, others of worn-out men missing legs and arms.

On the last page about the Great War, I found what I was looking for. It was a picture. Below it, I read "Three of our boys return from the trenches." Three young men stood together. The first one was kind of heavyset. The one in the middle had his right sleeve rolled up where his arm used to be. The third one had his arm around his friend.

I pulled the paper and pencil over and wrote down their names: Albert Loewan, Joe Warren and Roy Potter. I wrote the names in a list, like the list of dead men, and looked at the picture for a long time. The first man, except for the name, was Woody. I crossed out Albert Loewan's name and wrote "Woody." Then I looked at Joe Warren and the rolled-up sleeve. I wrote "Singing Man." I looked at Roy Potter for a while longer, trying my best to see the supervisor in Potter's face or eyes or body. But it wasn't the supervisor. Beside Roy Potter's name I wrote "Pots."

I stuffed the list into my pocket and walked to the door.

"Do you have a conclusion?" Jane Howe whispered.

"Yes, ma'am."

"Well? You can't leave me hanging."

"There were three of them," I said, and headed for home.

Along the road I thought about the picture, and how Woody looked just like his dad, and how Joe Warren was Singing Man, and how Roy Potter was Pots. I thought about the supervisor, too. I wondered if all four of them had been in Happy Valley or if only three had been there. And if it was only three, which three?

I would bet on Woody and Singing Man, but I would have to guess on the rest. I figured I would have to use sneakiness one more time.

That's when Dad pulled up beside me. He kicked the truck door open and bellowed, "Get in!"

I climbed in. The truck smelled like cigarette smoke and beer.

He ground the gears and pumped the clutch and ground the gears again. "Hold on, I think I found one," he called.

The truck jumped forward, and in a second we were swerving and jerking and bumping along the road. When we got to our lane, he was hanging on to the steering wheel with both hands and weaving around.

He turned into the lane and hit the gas. "Dammit," he said, "that's not the brake."

We roared down the lane and crashed into the caragana bushes. The doors flew open, and we both fell out.

I shook my head and got up.

Dad was lying on his back. "Look out for the caraganas!" he hollered.

I grabbed hold of him and hauled him up. He was pretty heavy and really drunk. Together we staggered into the house. It looked like me and Tim and Mom would get a little extra supper.

All the Kids Looked
Kind of Peaceful

Wednesday was test day. Mr. Parks sat on the corner of his desk and watched us come in. A pile of test papers sat beside him. He had one hand on the pile, and he was tapping his fingers like he did when he was waiting for the right answer to one of his questions.

Sammy walked past me. He didn't say anything to me or even look at me. He still smelled like stinky gopher tails. Woody didn't look at me either. He smelled like manure. Mary was smiling at Mr. Parks and everyone else, too. She smelled like flowers. Nobody said anything about my nose. I guess they were too worried about their tests.

I hated tests.

Mr. Parks looked up at the big clock on the wall above his desk and took a final look at the class. I could see he was counting or looking for empty desks that should have had a kid in them.

He got up and closed the door. That was it for any kid who was late — he would fail for sure. That was a pretty big rule.

Mr. Parks took an armload of tests and walked up and down the rows. He dropped one on each desk. Then he stood with his hands behind his back and rocked on his heels.

"Class, you have two hours to complete your test." He looked over his shoulder at the clock. The hands crept to nine o'clock. "You may begin," he said.

He sat in his chair and began his test stare. He never looked at any kid in particular. He looked at us all at the same time. His head moved slowly to the right, then slowly to the left. Sometimes it would stop in the middle, and sometimes it would change directions, but mostly it would move so slowly I couldn't tell which way it was going.

Mr. Parks was looking for even the smallest sign that a kid didn't understand something. And when someone got the confused look, Mr. Parks would get up slowly, quietly go over to the kid, and look down at him. Then he'd shake his head.

That was the only hint he would ever give.

The first question was about Galileo and the scientific method. It was easy. The rest of the questions were pretty tough, but I answered most of them.

At eleven o'clock, I turned in my test, grabbed my lunch, and headed for the caragana bushes that grew along the west edge of the school yard. I got as far as the hallway where all the kids were hanging around talking their after-test talk. "What did you get for question such-and-such?" and, "Oh, that's wrong."

I plugged my ears with my fingers and headed past them all. Before I got to the double doors leading outside, I found out I'd got question two wrong, and if Freddie Cooper's crying over the answer he'd given for question three was true, then I'd got that one wrong as well.

I got to the caragana bushes, ate my lettuce and salt and pepper sandwiches in little bites, pulled my knees up to my chest, and wrapped my arms around them. I just sat there watching the shadow of the Grayson water tower growing longer, creeping across the road till it was almost touching me. It was getting close to one o'clock, and all I had come up with was that Arthur hated me and three or maybe four *kaxtomo* had beat up Yellowfly.

Then the warning bell rang.

I took a long breath and slowly stood up.

A truck rumbled down the road that joined the highway to Grayson. Gravel crunched and popped under the wheels.

I walked to the roadside and looked. It was Mr. Norman. The engine made a little roar when he jammed in the clutch. The brakes let out a squeal. He stopped and stuck his hand out the side window.

"I found this in Happy Valley." In his hand was something wrapped up nice and neat in a clean white hankie. "Here. You'll know what to do with it. And by the way, next time you see Arthur, tell him he's as good a friend as a fellow could hope for in this life. I wouldn't be surprised if he feels the same way about you." He gave me a wink and drove off.

I stood holding the cloth in my upturned palm as if I was feeling the air for raindrops. It felt heavy. I figured it was a bunch of nickels.

I was wrong. It was Yellowfly's medal.

The ribbon was ironed smooth, and the metal was clean. I held it up high till the sun fell on its surface. And for the first time, I could see those words rising out of the metal on the cross that held the crown and the lion: "For Valour."

It was quite a sight.

The school bell rang, again.

The sun was blocked out by the Grayson water tower. I stood in its shadow and carefully folded up Yellowfly's medal and put it in my pocket.

The bell was fading. I was late.

I ran down the long sidewalk and hit the doors at full speed.

They banged open.

The janitor yelled.

When I got to the top of the stairs, Mr. Parks was standing holding the door. It should have been closed by now, but it wasn't. Mr. Parks had waited for me.

I ducked under his arm. My face felt hot.

"Tomato nose," Woody shouted.

I gave him a dirty look, and plunked myself in my seat.

"Settle down," Mr. Parks said.

"How come Samson isn't locked out?" Woody called. "How come he won't fail?"

"Mr. Samson will pass or fail this test on the strength or weakness of his character. Perhaps you should apply that standard to your own pursuits, Mr. Loewan."

"Huh?" Woody said.

I looked at the clock. Woody was right. It was after one. Mr. Parks had a sad look. I guess he was disappointed with me.

Mr. Parks gathered his armload of tests.

I picked up my pencil.

A few seconds later, he put a paper in front of me. It said, "Grade Six Reading and Writing Test." In the top corner, it said, "Name," and in the bottom corner it had two boxes. One said, "Pass," the other said, "Fail."

Woody's voice died away in my head. All that was left were those two words: "Pass" and "Fail."

I put my name on the top corner, turned the first page back, and pressed it down. I read the questions and answered them as best I could. They were the usual questions. "What did this person mean when she said that?" "What is the subject of this paragraph?" "What is wrong with this sentence?"

Finally, there was one question left. "On the next pages, write whatever you like. Just write well. Good luck." The rest of the pages were blank. It was the question Mr. Parks had put on the blackboard yesterday.

I'd forgotten all about it.

I must have looked confused because the next thing I knew Mr. Parks was standing beside me. He had his hand on my shoulder, but he didn't shake his head as a hint. He bent over and said very quietly, "You may write a true story."

When he said that, I knew what I was going to write. I folded the pages down nice and neat and started to write: "When we first saw it, I thought it was a dog, but Arthur said it was a man." I wrote and wrote and had just about wore out two pencils when Mr. Parks finally said, "Time's up."

I put my pencil down and looked around the room. All the kids looked kind of peaceful. I wasn't. I was mad, thinking about the last five days, all in one lump, and on paper. I didn't care if the men who beat up Yellowfly fought in the trenches or if they just fought in Happy Valley. I was going to find out who they were.

And I knew how I was going to do it.

He'd Be Tough

I pushed my way through the crowd of kids to the classroom door. Sammy was close behind me. He was pushing kids, too, and pulling on my shirt.

"What about Mary?" he asked.

"Get off my back."

"But you said you'd help."

"Go help yourself and stop being such a sissy."

Sammy's mouth fell open.

I turned on him and hollered right in his face, "I've got more important things to do than worry about you and your lovey-dovey."

Mr. Parks was holding the door for the slow kids. He gave me a stern look.

I gave him the same look back.

I was mad at everybody. And acting nice or being polite or even sneaky wouldn't help today, but I knew what would, and it was time to do it. I pulled the circle of tails out of my pocket and reached over and grabbed Woody.

He turned.

I jammed the gopher tails into his face and pushed him back toward the wall.

"Will Samson," Mr. Parks called, lunging for me.

He caught my shoulder.

I broke his grip.

Woody shook his head and spit through the faceful of gopher tails. "I'll kick your ass," he said.

"These look familiar? You thief."

"What?" Woody said, his eyes jerking quickly from the tails to my face. "Where the hell'd you get those?"

"Right where you dropped them, you ambushing son of a —"

A kid scrambled behind Woody.

I went to slam Woody's head into the wall.

Woody fell backward over the kid and landed with his feet in the air.

Mr. Parks grabbed me and spun me around.

I jerked, kicked at Woody, and caught the kid in the rear end.

"Ouch," the kid said.

Woody rolled over and pushed himself up the wall. "I'll get you, Samson!" he hollered.

"There'll be no getting by anyone," Mr. Parks said. He got a good grip on one of my arms and ducked as the other arm swung past his head. "Dammit, Will, stop flailing around."

I jerked in the direction he was pulling me and was loose.

Woody jumped for me.

Mr. Parks pushed me and caught Woody by the shirt collar. Woody's arms flew forward and his chin banged into his chest. "Hold on a damned minute, you two."

I could've sucker punched Woody right then, and it would've been okay by me and everyone else. But I didn't.

I held the circle of tails in his face and said as calmly as I could, "If you want these back, come and get them. I'll be waiting in Happy Valley where you dropped them, you Indian-ambushing son of a —"

"I'll get you good this time," he said, and spit.

"Tell your gang they won't be crossing the Rhine without a fight." I took a hard breath. The muscles in my jaw lumped up. "Tell the manure supervisor me and Arthur are waiting."

Woody had the same look as when he got washed over by Arthur's manure wagon. "That son of a bitch," he hollered, and jerked at Mr. Parks's grip. "I'll kick his ass so hard."

I made like I was done tormenting him. Then I turned back fast and shouted, "Tell Pots the only hero in Grayson is an Indian."

Mr. Parks had Woody with both arms now, one around his neck and the other around his chest.

Woody choked and cussed.

I made a whoop like the Indian boy had made in the barn and gave Woody one last rub with the tails. Then I said right in his face, "And tell him I've got Yellowfly's medal to prove it."

I pushed through the crowd of kids. Freddie Cooper had a big, dark spot on the front of his pants. Sammy was standing there with his mouth hanging open. Mary was near the wall, away from the crowd.

I stopped in front of Sammy. "What are you looking at?" I said. I spun the tails on my finger, rolled them neatly into my hand, and pointed at Mary, "Your lovey-dovey's over there."

Everybody was quiet except Woody. "I'll be there, Samson." He cussed. "And I'll kick your —"

Mr. Parks cuffed him in the back of the head.

Woody cringed.

"Watch yourself out there," Mr. Parks called to me.

I spun the tails again, gave Woody a smart grin, and started whistling, quietly at first because my lips were tough with fear, then louder. I turned and marched down the hall, spinning the tails and whistling. *Three German soldiers crossed the Rhine ...*

The Screaming, Flailing Madman

I stood in Happy Valley with the reserve behind me. My back felt hard and cold, as if Heavy Shield School had crawled up the road and was pushing me away from the reserve. But I couldn't feel Arthur anywhere. Maybe the brick and stone had made him cold, too. I gave myself a cuss and a hard slap and looked out at the lumps of buildings that made up the town. It helped some, but not enough to say I had anything like courage.

The beer parlor door opened and slammed closed.

Woody stepped out into the street and looked around. He adjusted his belt and, one by one, cracked his knuckles. I figured he would come ripping down the path like a wild man. He didn't. He just stood there.

I had to pee.

He looked past Gunther's gas station and grinned — like he was working up my fear.

I cracked my knuckles, too, but they didn't pop. They were soft and mushy like the rest of me.

The beer parlor door slammed again.

Woody looked over his shoulder.

Mr. Cooper's mechanic came out and walked up the street. He had a case of beer under each arm.

Woody crossed the street and headed down the path. His shoulders hung low from the weight of his arms. He passed the new cars and trucks, came up the rise of rocks, and crossed the tracks.

Rocks crunched under his feet.

A gopher jumped for cover.

I spread my legs a bit, got a good footing, and clenched my hands into hard fists.

He reached the rise that made the edge of Happy Valley and stepped in.

The air smelled of cigarette smoke and beer.

In a second, I'd figured out what to do. If he went to talk, I'd hit him. If he stopped, I'd hit him. If he did anything, I'd hit him. I'd throw the first punch. That was my only chance.

He was two steps from me when he broke his stride and slid his right foot, just a bit. It was a kick he had in mind.

"Hey!" I hollered, and pointed. "Is that your gang coming?"

He hesitated.

I threw a hard right for his nose.

Woody raised his shoulder to block the punch and kicked.

I caught him with everything I had square on the ear.

His kick glanced off my kneecap.

My punch spun him around in a full circle. He bent over and shook his head at the ground. He looked dazed, like he was trying to figure out the sound I'd put in his head.

Before he could shake off that punch, I swung a left at his other ear.

He lowered his head and turned.

My punch landed right on the top of his head. My arm went numb all the way to my elbow.

He lifted his head and grinned. "Your turn, Samson." He lurched and threw a punch.

It caught me flat on my nose. My head snapped back. "Jeez," I said. I grabbed my nose with my good hand, reeled, and fell backward into the dirt. My nose filled with blood and my eyes filled with tears. I was finished and I hadn't even seen his gang.

I looked through the cloud of water to see Woody flying through the air. He landed on me in a flurry of cusses and punches and kicks. I figured he would kill me, and if the cusses were even half true, he would do it slowly.

My head was full of the cusses and the sound of Woody's pounding fists when a scream came. First, I thought it was Arthur. But I knew it wasn't an Indian scream. It came from town.

Woody looked away for a second.

I got a knee under his ribs, pushed him over, and jumped up to run.

He grabbed me from behind.

I fell into the dirt again.

From Main Street, down the path, ran a screaming, flailing madman. It was Sammy Phillips. He hit the top of the rise and jumped. He missed us and landed face first in the dirt, got up, and jumped for Woody again. Sammy's arms looked like a windmill in a storm.

Woody caught about a hundred punches in the face before he got Sammy with an elbow in the neck.

Sammy made a gurgling sound and fell over.

I looked out from under Woody's boot and the mound of dirt pushed up to my face. From the corner of my eye, I could see Sammy holding his throat.

Then it was over.

I watched Woody's feet climb the rise and head back to town. He was finished with us. I pulled myself up and sat by Sammy. All I could see was the cloudy shape of Woody's back as he walked toward Grayson.

"I scared him off," Sammy said, and choked.

"Yeah, you showed him," I said. He'd also shown himself. And Mary. Everyone would be talking about how Sammy stood up to Woody.

"You got him good, Sammy."

He was almost crying from pride.

But there was something about Woody that didn't fit. How come he hadn't finished us off? Then I saw it. In the ambulance, someone was sitting and watching.

Woody got in and sat with the cloudy shape.

I could see clearer now. It was Pots.

I Got to Pee

Pots was glaring at me out the open driver's window when he pulled out from between two of Mr. Gunther's new Fargo trucks, turned left, and disappeared behind the Wheat Pool elevator.

I reached down and grabbed Sammy by the arm. "Come on, this thing isn't over yet." I walked with long, quick steps, then changed to a half run, always looking left to see where the ambulance had gone.

Sammy ran beside me. He was looking, too, but he didn't know what we were chasing Pots for. He figured we were still after Woody, which was partly true. He had his loose head checking left and right, then all the way back, then all the way forward. Sammy made a good lookout. On a check to the left, he punched one hand into the other.

"We'll show him — again," he said.

Sammy was surer of his chances than I was. He'd gained a lot of backbone from getting yelled at by me right in front of Mary and from getting nearly choked to death by Woody.

We crossed the three tracks and headed up the ramp and on through the big doors of the Wheat Pool. Mr. Norman was inside weighing grain. He waved. "Don't run across the scale," he said. "I can't afford to pay out your weight in flax."

We ran over the scale, right past Mr. Norman, and alongside the truck full of flax.

"Just making a shortcut," Sammy said.

"Me too," I said.

Sammy still had a big grin on his face even though he was talking around a choke. I never knew someone could be so happy from losing a fight.

"Sure, run over my scale. I don't want any trouble from such a rough-looking pair," Mr. Norman said, then laughed.

I just waved and headed past the truck.

"Who won?" he called.

"Will did," Sammy said.

"Sammy did," I said.

I could hear Mr. Norman talking over the pouring grain. "I'll have to subtract two kids' worth of flax from your load." Then he said something about being careful with those little ones, they can be a surprise.

Sammy gave him another wave that meant he knew Mr. Norman was talking about him. But we were already out of sight behind the truck.

That's when I saw the dray. It was parked behind a bunch of bushes that grew around the old station house. The horses were pointed away from downtown, and Watcher and His Brother sat with their backs to

Main Street, like they were waiting to give somebody a ride out of town.

Pots and Woody were stopped just across the street, pretty close to the bank. Pots was hollering cusses out the window. And Woody had his door open and was standing on the seat, his hands on the ambulance roof, his head above the red light. He was cussing worse than Pots.

But that didn't make Watcher or His Brother mad or anything — they just sat still and silent, facing the opposite direction, like they had done when they brought Arthur's mom and dad home from church.

Pots hit the gas. The ambulance shot rocks all the way to the foot of the ramp, and took off, sliding sideways down the alley behind the beer parlor, Woody hanging on to the red light with both hands, his door fully open, still cussing Watcher and His Brother.

"Are we going to beat up Pots, too?" Sammy asked with a nervous grin.

"Let's go," I said.

When we got to ground level, I couldn't see Watcher anymore. I couldn't see Pots and Woody either. Instead of following them, we walked down the beer parlor side of Main Street and headed toward Pots's insurance. At the hardware, I stopped to give Sammy a chance to get out of a worse fight.

"It's not your fight," I said.

"Mr. Parks said it's everybody's fight."

"When did he say that?"

"After Woody took off after you."

"He said you should fight Woody?"

"No. He said there's something wrong in Grayson. And that we should all fight it."

"How can we fight a thing?" I asked.

"Mr. Parks said we can start by not accepting it, by saying, even to yourself, that it's not right. When you feel strong enough, you can tell your brother or sister or friends or your mom or your dad that it's not right."

"All you have to do is say it?"

"That's what he said."

"Then how come you're here fighting, instead of just saying?"

Sammy looked in the big window of the hardware. His dad was standing at the counter. "Something's in me that can't be beat by saying. I've got to fight it."

I knew what Sammy was trying to beat. It was shame. The same kind of shame that had been felt in the barn at Heavy Shield School. And I knew what I was fighting for: I wanted Yellowfly to get some justice, and I wanted to prove I was a good enough friend to Arthur.

Sammy watched his dad work.

"He'll be mad if you're late," I said.

"I can help you. I've got fast hands. You saw how many times I hit Woody." He made a hard swallow.

"Are your hands just as fast when you use the telephone?"

"Of course."

"If you see Pots and Woody trying to kill me, call Mr. Parks and Mr. Norman and Jane Howe and everybody else."

"I'll sweep the floor up front so I can watch you."

I gave Sammy a slap on his shoulder and pointed at his dad. He was staring at us from the counter.

Sammy reached into his pocket, pulled out his hankie, and gave it to me. Then he turned and went into the hardware. Mixed in the folds of the hankie was a gopher tail.

Down the street, the ambulance was parked on an angle in front of Pots's insurance business. The whole Main Street was quiet, like the people were hiding.

I stuffed the gopher tail into my pocket with the circle of tails and headed down the street. As I went, I spit on Sammy's hankie and wiped the blood from my face. The hankie smelled like old gopher tails. I stopped on the street outside Pots's insurance. He sat with his back to the window.

"Hey!" I hollered. "Where's Woody?"

Pots just stared at the wall, like all this mess was none of his doing.

"Hey!" I hollered again.

A bang came from the back of the ambulance, and the back doors flew open.

Woody stepped out, stood by the door, and looked at me. One eye was swollen shut, and turning purple.

I guess that's what gave Sammy his nerve.

"Where'd you get that shiner?" I said.

"We're not done yet," he said.

Some cusses came from the ambulance. A pair of big army boots hung out the back, an empty sleeve hung over the bumper halfway to the ground.

"We'll show 'em all," Singing Man said.

He stumbled out and pulled himself along the open door, leaning on Woody with his good arm. He spit on the ground and cussed. "Where are they? I'll show 'em." He made a fist and almost fell over when he let go of Woody. Then he mumbled something about needing a drink, just to keep his whistle wet.

I thought about Dad. We were right beside Mr. Cooper's yard and the half-put-together swather. Dad should have been there watching the parts. Then I remembered the mechanic coming out of the beer parlor with an armload of beer.

Laughter came from behind Mr. Cooper's walls.

Dad was drunk.

"Hey," I hollered at Pots's picture window.

He turned his swivel chair around and stared at me over his half-glasses.

"Three to one is the way cowards fight," I said.

Pots got up, folded his hands behind his back, and walked over to the door. He looked down at me for a long second, then hooked the door open with his foot and stood in the opening. "Are you calling me out, Little Willy Yellowfly?"

I looked up from the street. He was bigger than me, and now I had to add the sidewalk and the floor of his office to his height. I lost my nerve.

"I just meant to say —" I stopped short as a sound came from up the street.

Just the sound of the rigging. The "Hee-aah!" came later.

Steel clanked on steel. Leather rubbed on flesh. Horses snorted. Hooves clopped.

I gave the old CPR house a quick glance as Watcher pulled back on the reins, stopping his team at the end of the street. The horses pulled against the reins, their muscles twitching. The two men sat with their feet on the hitch, Watcher rubbing his thumb on the oil-polished reins, His Brother staring right into my eyes, his arms resting on his knees, his hands hanging easy in the air.

Now it would be a fair fight.

I turned to Pots. "I want to know why you beat up Yellowfly."

"Yellowfly's comin'," Singing Man said. "I'll show 'im a real hero." He made a big, drunken, roundhouse punch and fell into the ambulance.

"What the hell," Pots said. "You good-for-nothing drunk."

"Get me up," Singing Man called.

Woody took his hand and pulled him up.

Singing Man stood and shook his head. His eyes were half closed. "Ya should'a let me do it," he said, and cussed Woody. "He wouldn't be coming back if I —"

"Shut up," Pots said.

I planted my feet and made two fists. "It'll take all three of you," I said, looking right at Pots. "And if that cowardly supervisor shows up, I'll take him on, too."

"Who's the supervisor that's comin'? You never tell me nothin', Pots," Singing Man said, then looked at Woody. "Where the hell's my beer? I was promised beer. If I gotta fight a supervisor, too, I'll need more beer." He took another wild swing, and Woody caught him before he fell.

"Whud I tell you," Pots said, stepped out into full view, and stood in the middle of the sidewalk.

"Hee-ahh!" Watcher screamed, and slapped the reins across the horses' backs.

The horses hit the tack so hard the hitch cracked like a rifle shot.

Then there came a warrior's cry over the sound of tack and hitch and leather and snorting. Hollering and screaming like hadn't been heard since the big No-Treaty said "No warriors."

I glanced up the street as the thunder grew. Watcher and His Brother were leaning forward, half standing on the hitch. In front of them was a pair of the wildest-looking horses I ever saw.

Hair stood up all over my body. It gave me more courage than my body could hold. There was only one of me and three *kaxtomo*, but I figured I could beat them.

While Woody was trying to hold up Singing Man, I took my shot. I jumped for Woody and, in midair, threw a kick. I missed and landed on my back. But Singing Man must've thought I was going for him because he lurched, knocked Woody down, and fell on him.

"I'll get that son of a —" Singing Man said, and stepped on Woody's hand as he tried to get up.

From under the pile, Woody cussed something to Jesus.

I reached up and gave Singing Man's empty sleeve a quick jerk.

He made three stumbling steps and fell into the street.

The horses let out a snort and the hitch clanked hard and Watcher hollered, "Whoa!"

Singing Man was on his back between the horses. He was cussing them and all their Indian ancestors.

The two horses were taking turns stepping on him.

"Look out, it's Yellowfly," Singing Man said to a horse. "Hit 'im. Hit 'im."

The horse he was talking to stepped on his foot.

The other one stepped on his empty sleeve.

Singing Man got loose and stood up.

The horses pushed together and held him there.

Singing Man turned blue and let out a big fart.

The horses snorted and shook their heads.

On his way down, he grabbed a horse's leg and held on. "Hit 'im again," he called. "He's still alive."

The other horse hit him again.

There was a bunch more cussing. Singing Man crawled out from between the horses and right under the ambulance.

"Get him, Woody!" Pots hollered.

Woody stomped on my foot and hit me hard in the stomach.

All my air jumped out. I bent over, making little squeaking sounds.

Woody lifted my head by my hair and wound up with his right.

I tried to close my eyes, but they wouldn't close. There was somebody coming out from behind the ambulance door. I squeaked again.

Sammy jerked Woody's punching arm and spun him around. Woody was still turning when Sammy let go with a punch that traveled all the way from the beginning of grade six. He caught Woody in his only good eye.

"There," Sammy said. "Now you've got a set."

Woody landed in the dirt, his hands over both eyes. Sammy could punch him all day. If he wanted to.

My squeak let go, and I sucked in most of the air in Grayson.

"I gave him the first one, too," Sammy said, grinning.

"I thought you were going to —" I caught another breath and let it out.

"— use my fast hands on the telephone?" Sammy said, and motioned up the street.

Out of the corner of my eye, I saw Mr. Norman disappear down the long ramp. Jane Howe stuck her head out the library door. Mr. Wong looked out his café window. Inside Cooper's machine shop, the laughter had died down to nothing.

Watcher spoke in a very low voice. "One left," he said.

I knew then it wasn't just a fight. Watcher could have climbed off the wagon and beat all three. He could've done it easy. But if Watcher got into the fight, he would go to jail and Pots would go free, just like what had happened for a hundred years. Just like Arthur had said. That wouldn't be the kind of justice I wanted for Yellowfly, and that wouldn't get a friend back. And I knew now, too, why Watcher was there. It was to give me courage.

Pots was still standing on the sidewalk with his hands folded behind his back, not saying a word, just watching. He'd go to jail if he hit a kid. That was our only chance, and it'd have to happen fast, before the town people stopped him.

I turned on him. "You did it. You beat Yellowfly. A man who was a hero."

He just stood there.

"You'd never get a medal," I said. "You're not brave. You're a coward."

Woody was leaning back over the front fender of the ambulance. He was rubbing his eyes, trying to get the swelling down far enough so he could see through the fog.

Mr. Norman was running down the middle of Main Street. The wind made by his own running made it look like he might start flying at any minute. Jane Howe was standing in the street now. Mr. Wong was coming through his door. Mr. Phillips turned the corner in the alley behind Dad's piles of red parts. Noise came from inside Mr. Cooper's shop. The Mountie's siren screamed from the far side of town.

For courage, I thought of Yellowfly's medal. I touched my pocket. I could feel heat in it even under all its layers of cloth, like it was alive, because it had been worn by a hero.

"Yellowfly won the Victoria Cross." I took a breath. "For valor. He's the only hero I know. He's my hero." I gave Pots a hard look and spit on the ground at his feet. "And I know who you are, too. I read about you in a book."

Pots smiled like he was remembering the story.

"It said 'three of our cowards return from the trenches.' You must've had some Indians to help you beat the Germans in those damned trenches, because cowards can't do nothing alone but sneak around and sucker punch real heroes. I know who you are. You're *Kaxtomo*."

All I remember is the look on Pots's face, the ugly hateful look, and the bat he had behind his back, and the way he swung it at my head, and Sammy pushing me from behind so the bat hit my shoulder and bounced off, catching me below the eye. And the jumble of voices that filled my head, the voices from Blackfoot Crossing, where Treaty Number 7 was signed in 1877.

Chief Crowfoot and Colonel Macleod were there. So were Yellowfly and Arthur, and they were yelling to Crowfoot, "Don't sign it till the white man can hold the promise in his heart — till he can say *waahkoomohsi*."

And over those words came the sound of Watcher snapping the reins and the horses snorting and the dray rolling down the street, to a clump of poplars where the men could sit and watch the town.

Then came Mr. Parks's voice. "Hey, what's going on there?"

And Jane Howe. "Oh, good God."

And Mr. Phillips. "Sammy!"

And Mr. Wong. "It was Pots."

And Dad cussing. "Pots, you son of a bitch."

Then Sergeant Findley. "Hold on there, Jim Samson." And, "You can't do this to white people, Pots."

And Pots hollering. "It was those Indians — the ones on the dray."

And everyone saying, "Don't listen to him. It's a lie."

I felt thin fingers on my neck and heard Mr. Norman's voice. "For God's sake, men, make room for the doctor."

Then came Dr. Wilcox's voice. "Can you hear me, son?"

I just watched as he dug in his bag. I could've talked, I just didn't bother trying.

"Can you hear me?" He looked into my eyes, then he shook a small bottle, opened it, and stuck it under my nose.

I choked and jerked my head away. It was the worst horse pee I'd ever smelled.

"Good lad," he said, and looked over to the cloudy people. "I've seen worse at the rodeo. But I'll run him over to the Indian hospital and take some X-rays of that shoulder and that head. But if he's half as thickheaded as his father, he'll be just fine."

Everybody was trying to get me up or hold my hand or give me a drink or a ride home from the hospital or something.

I just mumbled, "Mr. Gunther's green Coke."

And Sammy was off.

Mr. Parks and Mr. Norman were standing by Pots's door, arguing with Sergeant Findley.

"You have to charge him," Mr. Norman said.

"He assaulted a boy," Mr. Parks said.

"We have witnesses," Mr. Norman added.

"Damn the two of you," Findley said, and kicked his car. "Get in!" he roared at Pots.

"Like hell," Pots said.

I sat up in time to see the sergeant slam his car door behind Pots. Pots was lying in a heap in the back seat. A second later, Singing Man went flying into the back seat, too. Then it was Woody's turn.

"There, Norman," Findley hollered. "Are you happy now?"

"It's a start," Mr. Norman said.

I was seeing six of everybody. I didn't like it much till I saw six Sammys running back from Gunther's gas station carrying six eye-popping green Cokes. Sammy snapped open the Coke with his jackknife and set it in my lap.

I took a swig. The six of everybody got kind of frosty looking. I took some more swigs.

Then Dad and Sammy helped me up.

Jane Howe gave a little cheer.

I gave her a wave.

I turned to Sammy and gave him his hankie and the one gopher tail. Then I dug the circle of gopher tails out of my other pocket. When I handed them to him, they weren't a circle anymore. They'd come untied in my pocket. "Here," I said. "I don't need them anymore." Then I got a funny feeling inside.

"What is it?" Dad asked and leaned over to hear me.

"I got to pee."

Dad gave me a big wink. "Me, too."

Together we staggered into Cooper's yard. Behind the swather, where nobody could see, we peed on Pots's wall.

Pass or Fail

Thursday was the last day of the last week of grade six. Mom had said I should stay home and let my bruises heal. I couldn't. I had to get my report card. And I still had some unfinished business.

I was daydreaming about the Calgary Stampede when I got to my desk. Tom Ward's chuckwagon had just won its heat. I was hanging over the rail as he rode past. He lifted his hat and waved it at me. I waved back.

Mr. Parks smiled and waved to me.

I was kind of embarrassed.

Mr. Parks had a pile of brown envelopes sitting in the middle of his desk. I expect it was the same all over the country: teachers sitting, piles of brown envelopes, scared kids.

Sammy came in last. He walked nice and easy and half stopped at Mary's desk. He was acting kind of lovey-dovey.

"Mmm, you smell nice," Mary said.

Sammy walked slowly between the rows of desks and acted like he never heard her. But I knew he had. He grinned at me when he passed. His hair was combed neat, like he was going to church, and he smelled like his dad's aftershave. He sat by his window and didn't even open it.

There was no sign of Woody. Too bad. It would've been nice for all the kids to see what Woody got for pushing Sammy too far. But I expect they knew. And I suppose it didn't matter even if they didn't know, because Sammy knew.

Mr. Parks started calling our names.

And one by one we got our report cards.

There were screams and yahoos from all over the school. Some kid from grade five ran down the hall yelling, "I passed! I passed!" He was probably the dumbest kid in grade five, who got the worst day of the year turned back into the best.

I listened to all the happiness and all the sadness.

Then everyone was gone but me and Mr. Parks. "Will Samson," he called, holding a brown envelope in his hand. "Good luck, Will."

"Thanks," I said.

He was smiling at me when I left. When I got to the door, he said, "Aren't you going to open it?"

I stopped but didn't turn around. "Yeah, I'll look," I said. "Someplace where nobody will see me cry."

"You won't have to cry," he said.

"Maybe I'll have to sing and dance."

"That is certainly possible, but you'll have to open the envelope to find out."

I looked at the spot where I'd pushed Woody up against the wall, where I'd been mean to Sammy in front of Mary. I fiddled with my report card. "Yesterday," I said after a long pause, "did you send Sammy after me?"

"Sammy went because he had to. Just like you did what you had to."

"What's wrong in Grayson?"

"Less than there used to be."

In that moment I thought about all the mean things I'd said about Indians in my life. It seemed to me that there was still lots wrong in Grayson. Then I thought about yesterday. "Thanks for not locking me out and making me fail like Woody wanted."

"I made that rule for all my students to live by," he said. "But sometimes there is something more important than rules."

"Sammy had to fight, even though he knew fighting is against the rules."

"As did you, Will."

I thought about Woody and Singing Man and Pots. "What's wrong in Grayson?" I asked again.

"We lack courage." Mr. Parks smiled his nice smile. "But not as much as we used to."

I walked into the hall and passed all the things that were grade six, all the scuffs, and all the missing paint. At the end of the hall where grade six ended, I stopped and opened the envelope. Next to "Reading and Writing" there was a big fat A. And on the back page it said "Pass."

I let out a scream and jumped so high I nearly touched the ceiling.

Unfinished Business

I stuffed my report card into my pocket and headed downtown. Along the way, I took my Stampede money out of my pocket and counted it. I had managed to save seventy-eight cents, mostly from selling gopher tails. I put my hand back into my pocket and held the money for a while longer.

I liked how it felt.

When I got to the church, I sat on the front steps and looked out over the town. It looked the same as it ever did, quiet and peaceful. Some people moved around slowly. Nobody was ever in much of a hurry in Grayson.

I leaned against the big wooden doors and rested my head. I could hear the songs like it was Sunday. Jesus was in every sentence, like always. There was nobody in the church, I knew that. It was just those leftover words that got stuck in the wood, and the plaster and the glass, and maybe some even got stuck in me.

I looked downtown. Heat waves filled the streets. It was going to be another hot one.

I jingled the money as I walked past Frankie's store. I thought about Singing Man, but instead of singing the German-soldiers song, I was singing one of the Jesus songs.

I walked up to the open space where Dad was working. I waved. "Hi, Dad," I said.

He waved without looking around and said something about potatoes.

The door was closed to Pots's insurance. I wondered if he was in jail. In my mind, I heard one more holler from Pots, like it was from inside his office. "Well, if it isn't Little Willy Yellowfly." Then he laughed. I figured he would be in my head for a while.

I touched my pocket where Yellowfly's medal was. Then I took a breath and headed up the street.

Next stop was Phillips's hardware. Mr. Phillips was behind the counter. Sammy wasn't there. I figured he and Mary were someplace being lovebirds.

I walked up to Mr. Phillips and put all my money on the counter. "I'd like to buy some gopher tails."

"I thought you were the seller, not the buyer," Mr. Phillips said.

I just stared at my money.

"Okay." He pulled the old shoe box from under the counter and poured out about a hundred tails.

I expect the circle of fifty tails I'd given back to Sammy was in there mixed with the rest.

I counted out seventy-eight cents.

Mr. Phillips counted out seventy-eight tails.

That was it for my Stampede money. I stuffed the tails into my pocket. They still stunk, but I didn't mind.

Mr. Phillips dinged open the cash register and took out two nickels. "You've been a good friend to Sammy," he said, and pushed the nickels across the counter.

"I like Sammy," I said, and pushed the nickels back to Mr. Phillips. "I'd like ten more tails, please."

"You're a funny one," he said, and counted out ten tails.

I walked down the path past Mr. Gunther's new cars and trucks. Mr. Norman was standing at the top of his ramp. He was leaning on his grain broom, watching the town.

I gave him a wave.

He waved back.

I crossed the tracks and headed into Happy Valley. It looked like a dirt hollow, like nothing had ever happened here. I dragged my feet as I walked through the heavy dust, making cuts in the ground, and turned down the path that ran alongside the railway tracks to Arthur's house.

Lots of gophers were out. I thought about how much money I could get for their tails. There was always plenty of gophers — lots of money for a kid to make. But I didn't much care for snaring gophers anymore.

I sat on the rail and looked at Arthur's house. The smoke from the cook-fire drifted across the narrow strip of railway land and gathered around me like the cloud of tiny flies that had settled over Arthur the day we found Yellowfly. All around, the air smelled of poplar smoke and a little bit of cooking bannock.

I looked back the way I had come, through the layer of heat waves and smoke that floated over the tracks, and on down the two lines of shining steel — wandering forever east until it became a single thing. A steel river. Separating the Blackfoot from everything that was white.

Arthur's grandpa came out and went to the outhouse.

I sat there, watching and waiting. I didn't really know what I was expecting. Maybe nothing.

The old man came out and walked slowly back to the house. He didn't see me sitting there. I was ready to wave and go over if he called. But he didn't.

I figured Arthur should've been back home from Heavy Shield School by now. Maybe he'd failed grade six and had to stay there forever, or maybe he was inside the house watching me. I sat there anyway and smelled the bannock. It reminded me of chopping wood. I wondered if Arthur was still mad at me for what Woody had done and what the supervisor had done. I thought about the No-Treaty. This time it was Crowfoot who was telling Macleod what to put in the Treaty. "No truth. No friends."

I started back home. The heat was worse than ever, but that didn't matter, I wasn't thinking about anything but Indians and my unfinished business.

The watcher gophers were there, keeping an eye out for danger. They were watching me, like they always did. This was where I did most of my snaring. I sat and watched back. After a while, even the watchers went about their gopher business.

I went to their hole and their big pile of dirt. I knelt and made a groove in their dirt pile like I'd done when I'd hid my snare. I reached into my pocket and pulled out one of the tails and put it into the groove and covered it with dirt.

The watchers were looking at me again.

I went to the next hole and did the same. I did it over and over, and at some, I buried two tails, where I remembered I'd snared two gophers. I could have done it with my eyes closed. The meanness I did to them was so much a part of me that I didn't even have to think about it to remember.

I did that till I was out of tails.

Now all the gophers were standing, not just the watchers, but the mom gophers and the little gophers. They were all around me.

"That's all the money I had."

They looked at me like it wasn't enough.

"I'm sorry I hurt you." I turned in a circle and said it again and again till I figured they'd all heard.

Friendship

Dad was cooking flapjacks on the woodstove. The skillet was big and black and would cook four the size of dinner plates. He had it loaded, and there was already a pile as big as a milk bucket sitting in the middle of the table.

"That's plenty for now," Mom said.

"I've got to finish up the batter." Dad poured the remaining batter in the middle of the skillet, then grinned at Mom.

Mom looked away and bowed her head. "Dear Lord, thank you for this bounty." She opened one eye and peeked at the stack. "And thank you for protecting my youngest from the evil of this world. And if you could help my eldest child with his cooking, I'd appreciate it."

Dad flipped a spoonful of batter at Mom.

Mom ducked and the batter sailed over her shoulder.

Me and Tim snickered and went back to eating. We were eating as fast as we could. Partly, we were racing to see who could eat the most; but mostly, we were trying to get full before the big one got cooked.

"Leave some for me." Dad grinned.

"Good Lord," Mom said. "There's enough for a camp full of starving lumberjacks."

Dad lifted his batter spoon.

Mom wagged her finger.

Sometimes Dad made soda biscuits, and sometimes he made flapjacks. Sometimes he made them because he wanted to, but mostly he made them as a way of saying sorry to Mom for getting drunk the night before.

Mom looked at my nose and my eye. "You should buy your insurance someplace else, and never mind Pots," she said to Dad.

"Mr. Cooper said he's going to switch to Gladstone over in Bosworth," Dad said. "I'll switch the truck tomorrow."

"Jane Howe has a new Dodge car," I said. "Maybe she needs insurance, too."

"I'll stop by the library on Monday," Dad said.

"I didn't like Pots before, when he was mean to Indians," she said. "I like him even less now."

"Nobody likes him anymore." Dad lifted the flapjack and checked it. "Not since he beat up a kid," he said, and gave me a wink.

"Will the Mounties do anything to Pots?" Mom asked.

"Findley? Hell, no. But it's not up to him now. The judge will decide, thanks to Parks and Norman. They're pretty good witnesses. And there were others," Dad said.

"I heard there were Indians there on an old dray," Mom said.

"I didn't see any," Dad said. "Mind you, I'd had a few." He winked at Mom.

Mom just shook her head.

"What about Woody?" Tim asked. "What'll happen to him?"

"Nothing," Dad said. "He's just a kid."

"And Joe Warren?" Mom asked.

"There's no law against getting half killed by two horses," Dad said, checking his flapjack again.

It was just about ready to flip.

"But all three attacked Yellowfly," Mom said.

Dad took a big breath. I figured he would get mad when it wasn't his idea to talk about an Indian. But he didn't say anything right away. He just kept checking his giant flapjack.

"Jim," Mom said.

"Dammit," Dad said. "I said I'll go someplace else for insurance."

"But Yellowfly," Mom said.

"He's alive, isn't he? If he wants more, he'll just have to wait."

"Wait for what?"

"For people to change."

Dad put the big flapjack on his plate. His plate disappeared. He gave his lips a slow all-over licking. He did it to me first, then to Tim. He was trying to get us to forget about Yellowfly. He was a pretty good dad sometimes.

Mom looked away from Dad. She was trying not to laugh. "The boys are done school," she said.

Dad looked at Tim. "You figure you passed?"

"Sure," Tim said from under a swallow.

"How 'bout you?" Dad asked me.

"I did okay," I said, and took a big bite.

"All I expect of them is to pass," Mom said.

"Passing is good enough. Can you pass the syrup, Mom?" Dad asked and grinned.

Mom would've shook her head again if she figured it would've done any good.

Dad ate the giant flapjack, then started on four more.

I finished up the two I was working on. Now I was tied with Tim. I reached for two more.

"Aw," Tim said, then took two more himself.

And the race was on. In a while, Tim was a green color, but he'd won. I was green, too. I'd lost. And Dad was just green. Mom was shaking her head and looking the other way.

Dad wiped his mouth with his sleeve and put his hands beside his plate. His sleeve soaked up some syrup that got spilled on the table. He let out a big burp, and me and Tim snickered.

Mom looked crossly at him. "Jim," she said.

He pushed back his chair and rolled a cigarette. He lit it, picked a piece of tobacco off the tip of his tongue, and started talking.

I thought about the barn supervisor at Heavy Shield School, how nobody could prove he was part of Pots's gang, how hearing that from me made Mr. Norman red-faced with anger. Then when Mr. Wilcox drove me home from the Indian hospital after taking X-rays of my head and shoulder, I saw Mr. Norman's pickup parked at the train station. The barn supervisor had an old suitcase in his hand, and Mr. Norman had a hold of one of the supervisor's ears, twisting it nearly off as he marched him down the platform and pushed him into the passenger car with his foot and closed the door on him. I'd asked Dr. Wilcox where the train was headed. He said I didn't have to worry about anybody on that one — it was one of those one-way trains. Then he gave me a wink.

That's when I heard the snort coming from outside.

Dad swallowed a mouthful of smoke and said, "Darn, was that a horse?"

There was another snort followed by the sound of leather rubbing on flesh, metal clanking on metal, and somebody calling, "Whoa."

"That's a horse," Mom said. She went to the window and looked down. "There's two of them, and they're hitched to a dray. And there's three Indians sitting on it."

"What are they doing?" Dad asked.

"Nothing, they're just sitting there."

"Tim, go see what they want," Dad said.

"I'll go," I said, and jumped up.

Mom was still standing at the window. "That's a couple'a sorry-looking horses."

I walked through the porch and headed outside. I had my hand pushed hard against Yellowfly's medal. Even through all the layers of cloth, I could still feel "Valour." When I got to the bottom of the stairs, I saw the two horses. Then I saw Watcher and His Brother. And there at the back of the dray, sitting with his legs hanging over the edge, was Arthur.

We didn't speak. It seemed like we didn't even breathe.

There, I thought about Woody and the supervisor at Heavy Shield School. And I remembered saying some mean things to Indians myself. I knew I had tried a hundred times to say to Arthur I was sorry. I also knew even a million times wouldn't be enough. Not for me or Dad or the town or the past hundred years. I could say I was sorry for the rest of my life and it still wouldn't make up for meanness in the first place.

I remembered what Sammy had said, what he said Mr. Parks had told him. And that's what I said. "I don't accept meanness. It's not right." I said it so anybody who was listening could hear. I turned to our kitchen window. Tim and Mom and Dad were staring down. I said it to Watcher and His Brother.

Then I looked at Arthur. I thought about Chief Crowfoot and the big No-Treaty, how Arthur had said it was in the white man's nature to make a promise, then later find a way around it. I figured Indians thought the No-Treaty was a promise that was never kept. My throat got thick as I thought about the Blackfoot word that Arthur said Macleod had tried to say to Crowfoot, but couldn't. I had to take a big breath and swallow.

"No meanness," I said. "*Waahkoomohsi.*"

"You promise me," Arthur said. "In my own language? You must'a been practicing that one for a long time."

I nodded. "About a hundred years."

They were all watching me now, those sitting on the dray, those standing at our kitchen window, and those hitched to the front of the dray.

I took another big breath and pulled Yellowfly's medal out and gave it to Arthur.

He pressed it tight in his hand, then put it into his pocket. He didn't have to look to know what it was.

Watcher leaned back and slapped the planks.

I jumped on, and in a second the horses were huffing and puffing. We crossed the lane and turned down the road. Everybody was quiet. After a long while, I made a sign. It wasn't a real sign. It was just a made-up one. But nobody seemed to mind, because they all understood what I was saying.

Watcher nodded and made the same sign.

So did His Brother.

Then Arthur looked at me and held a closed fist to his chest, then he crossed his arms and held them both over his heart, like I had just done. I knew he was saying what I was saying: You're as good a friend as a fellow could hope for in this life.

ACKNOWLEDGMENTS

To my agent, Joanne Kellock, thank you for your firm guidance. Thank you to Kids Can Press for seeing something more than work in a humble first novel, and to Charis Wahl, editor and kind heart, thank you for turning all that work into a tolerable, if not enjoyable, experience.

Thank you, Barbara Smith, for your friendship and faith in a fellow writer, and thank you, Ven Begamudré, for your hard work, tolerance and friendly pen while Writer in Residence at the University of Alberta. Thank you to the Writers Guild of Alberta and the Alberta Foundation for the Arts for running and sponsoring the Alberta Writing for Youth Competition.

To Mom and Dad and my gang of brothers and sisters, thank you for your years of story material, inspiration and, of course, love. Thank you to the good people of Gleichen, Alberta, for your quiet courage. And thank you to the Blackfoot people I have known, with special thanks to Mark Wolfleg and his family and Roy Stimson and his family — thank you for the glimpse into your brave past, your good humor and your friendship.

And to Teya Rosenberg, English teacher, without whom I might still be hiding from myself. Thank you for lighting the dark place where fear defeats determination. Thank you for all those wonderful words. And thank you for showing me my heart.